This book
belongs to

Claire

J8
.50

4

FABER-CASTELL

since 1761

Penny the Pencil has a proud heritage. She is made by the leading pencil manufacturer in the world, Faber-Castell. The Faber-Castell family have been making pencils for eight generations. It all started in a small workshop in Germany in 1761 and now the company employs 5,500 people worldwide. The company is run by Count Anton Wolfgang von Faber-Castell.

Faber-Castell is a company with great flair and vision. It is in the *Guinness Book of Records* for creating the world's tallest pencil at almost twenty metres high and has also made the most expensive pencil ever. The Grip 2001 pencil brings together these elements of design, quality and innovation. It has won many international awards. With its unique soft grip zone and comfortable triangular shape it has become a worldwide classic.

EILEEN O'HELY

PENNY tHE PENCIL

Illustrated by Nicky Phelan

MERCIER PRESS

MERCIER PRESS
Douglas Village, Cork
www.mercierpress.ie

Trade enquiries to Columba Mercier Distribution,
55a Spruce Avenue, Stillorgan Industrial Park,
Blackrock, County Dublin

1 85635 475 X

10 9 8 7 6 5 4 3 2 1

Mercier Press receives financial assistance from
the Arts Council/An Chomhairle Ealaíon

Printed and Bound by J. H. Haynes & Co. Ltd, Sparkford

Contents

For Nova

Ralph

Sarah

Main Characters

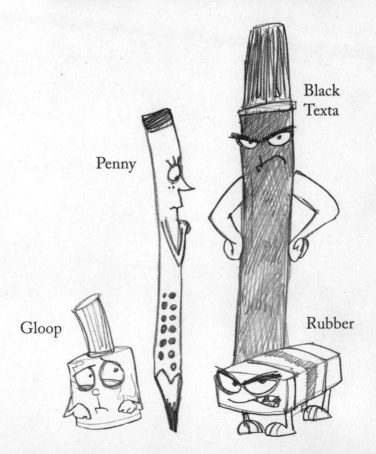

Penny

Black
Texta

Gloop

Rubber

chapter 1

McPaper's Books and Stationery Supplies

It was the end of the summer holidays.
McPaper's Books and Stationery Supplies
was full of customers. Mothers and
children, eager to go back to school, were
buying exercise books, biros, pencils, rulers,
rubbers, bottles of glue, sticky-tape,
scissors, pencil-cases, textas, folders and
textbooks. Not only were the mothers and
children excited (and of course Mr
McPaper, who hadn't had a single customer
all summer!), but the items for sale in
McPaper's Books and Stationery Supplies

were absolutely jumping for joy. Finally, after sitting on the shelves all summer, with nobody even walking into the shop, they were being picked up by smiling children and thrust into shopping bags.

A little girl called Sarah, wearing a blue ribbon in her hair, was the only child in the shop without her mother. Sarah lived with her grandmother who was very poor.

'Granny, Granny! Look at that lovely, big box of coloured pencils! There are twenty-four and they look so pretty. Can we buy them? Please?' begged Sarah. Sarah's grandmother looked in her purse and frowned. She only had twelve euro left and they still had to buy Sarah a dictionary.

'Let's have a look at the dictionaries first,' she said, taking Sarah firmly by the hand and steering her away from the coloured pencil section.

'Oh, look!' said Sarah as they got to the
aisle where the dictionaries were for sale.
'Mr McPaper is having a special! If you buy
one of these coloured dictionaries then you
get a free pencil! I'd like the blue one!'

Sarah pointed to the last blue dictionary

sitting on the top shelf, which was too high for her to reach. Sarah's grandmother, who was only a little taller than Sarah, reached up to the top shelf and picked up the dictionary. She turned it over and looked at the price tag. It cost nine euro. They wouldn't be able to afford both the dictionary and the coloured pencils. She handed the book to Sarah.

'Wow!' said Sarah, opening the dictionary. 'Even the words are in colour! This is a cool dictionary!' she said, then quickly cupped her hand over her mouth in case anyone from school was nearby and had heard her say that a schoolbook was cool.

Sarah quickly took the dictionary to the cash register, forgetting all about the

coloured pencils. Sarah's grandmother breathed a sigh of relief, paid Mr McPaper for the dictionary, and walked Sarah out of the shop before she had time to remember the coloured pencils.

On the way out, Sarah bumped into her best friend Ralph, who was shopping with his mother.

'Hi Ralph! Look at the dictionary we just bought. It's blue and the words are in colour! And look – it comes with a free pencil!' said Sarah, showing Ralph her new purchase.

'That's exactly what you need, Ralph,' said Ralph's mother. 'Something to help you with your spelling.'

Ralph winced. He knew he wasn't very good at spelling (or sums or anything else at school for that matter), but it was embarrassing for his mother to keep mentioning it in front of people.

'I'd prefer a red one ...' mumbled Ralph, looking at his shoes. Sarah also looked at the ground, not knowing what to say.

'Well, I'm sure you have a lot to do, so we won't keep you,' said Sarah's grandmother, noticing that the children had grown quiet. 'Come along, Sarah.'

'Tsk, tsk,' said Dictionary, a wise, old red dictionary, to the free pencil that was sticky-taped to it. They'd both been observing the conversation in the shop doorway by peering over the shelf of atlases in front of them. 'Whatever is the world coming to? Choosing a dictionary based on its colour, rather than the quality of the definitions within ...'

'Oh, cheer up,' said Penny Pencil. 'Now that all the blue dictionaries have been sold, someone who likes red will come along and buy us! Maybe even that little boy in the doorway.' Penny tried to turn her body to get a better look at the people walking up and down the aisle, but it is very difficult to move when you're sticky-taped to a big, red dictionary.

'Somebody who likes red will buy us indeed!' snorted Dictionary. 'Haven't you learned anything I taught you all summer?'

'What?' said Penny, a little distracted as she watched the customers hopefully.

'Humans!' continued Dictionary disdainfully. 'All of them searching for the meaning of life. All they have to do is pick me up, turn to page 427, and they'll find it …'

Penny was used to Dictionary rabbiting on about the meaning of different words. She'd actually learned quite a lot from him over the summer – what different words meant and how to spell them. But today wasn't like all the other summer days, sitting on the shelf watching people pass by the shop without ever stepping inside. Today the shop was full of people, and Penny was sure that soon a little girl (or boy) would point to her and Dictionary and ask their mother if they could buy them.

'Look, Dictionary,' said Penny, straining at her sticky-tape to look at the boys and girls walking along the aisles. 'Somebody will buy us any minute now! Maybe that little girl with the pink ribbon in her hair, or that little boy carrying the blue truck …'

But before Penny could finish her sentence there was a sharp jerk and she was almost blinded by bright lights.

'What's happening?' she said, trying to wriggle close to Dictionary for safety, even

though the sticky-tape was already holding
her on tightly. Suddenly everything went
dark again, and all she could hear was
the sound of Dictionary laughing.

'What are you laughing about?
What's so funny?' said Penny
angrily. As it was, she was feeling
a little seasick, and whenever
Dictionary laughed he always
shook a little, which made
Penny feel quite queasy indeed!
'Would you stop it?'
demanded Penny as the shaking
got worse and worse.

'I have stopped,' said Dictionary,
but the shaking was still there.

'Then why are we still shaking?
And why is it so dark? Where have
the atlases gone?' asked Penny,
feeling very sick and very frightened.

'I'd say,' began Dictionary in the reassuring voice he used with Penny when she got confused about the meaning of a particularly long word, 'that the atlases are still on the shelf, while we are in a shopping bag on our way to the check-out!'

'You mean ...' began Penny, so excited that she forgot that she was feeling sick.

'Yes. Someone is buying us!' said Dictionary. And even though he was a wise, old dictionary, Penny thought he sounded a little bit excited too.

All of a sudden there was a loud bang and the shaking stopped. Dictionary groaned a little.

'Be careful, Ralph!' said a woman's voice. 'You don't want to have to buy Mr McPaper a new counter, do you?'

'Sorry, Mr McPaper,' said a little boy's voice.

'Oh, that's all right, Ralph,' said Mr McPaper chuckling. 'Lots of books have landed on the counter this morning. What are we buying today?' he asked, reaching into the shopping bag.

Penny felt a jerk and suddenly she was blinded by the bright ceiling lights again.

'Ah! One of the red dictionaries. The blue ones are more popular,' continued Mr McPaper.

'Oh, red's my favourite colour!' said Ralph, and before Penny and Dictionary were put back in the shopping bag, Penny caught a glimpse of a little boy with red hair, green eyes and freckles, wearing a red T-shirt.

12

'We're not buying the dictionary because it's red, Ralph. We're buying it to help you with your spelling!' said Ralph's mother firmly.

'Having trouble with spelling, are we?' said Mr McPaper, looking at Ralph over the top of his glasses.

Ralph looked at the ground and nodded his head.

'I bet your spelling's not so bad. How do you spell lollipop?' asked Mr McPaper.

'L-O-L-L-I-P-O-P,' said Ralph.

'See?' said Mr McPaper, smiling and giving Ralph a red lollipop. 'You know how to spell the important words at least! Now enjoy yourself at school tomorrow.'

Ralph's mother paid Mr McPaper for Dictionary and Penny, and picked up the shopping bag. The shaking began again but this time Penny didn't feel seasick. She was happy to be going home with a little boy, who would put her in his pencil-case, take her to school, and write with her. And she was going to do her best to help him learn to spell.

chapter 2

The Pencil-case

When Ralph got home, he ran straight up to his room and took Penny and Dictionary out of the shopping bag. He peeled Penny and the sticky-tape off Dictionary, and shoved Penny into his pencil-case. Then he opened Dictionary and started trying to learn to spell.

Penny poked her head out of the pencil-case to see what was going on, when a loud voice boomed:

'You there! New pencil. Come away from the zip. What's your name?'

Penny turned around slowly. A big,

black, important-looking texta
with the word 'Autocrat' written
down its side was frowning at her.
'Didn't you hear me? I asked
you your name,' boomed the
big black texta.

'P-P-Penny,' said Penny
very quietly.

Penny heard her name repeated
a few times. She saw coloured
pencils, crayons, highlighters and
textas all looking at her curiously.

'Have you come from McPaper's?'
demanded Black Texta.

'Y-y-yes,' said Penny, feeling very unsure
of herself.

'Any other biros, pencils, crayons,
permanent markers, highlighters, rubbers,
etc come with you?'

Penny had to think for a moment.

'No. Only Dictionary.'

'Dictionary? Hey, Amber - what's a dictionary?' whispered a short green pencil called Jade to the tall orange pencil beside it.

'It's a book,' said Amber, the orange pencil, laughing under her breath.

'Oh! A book!' said Jade, laughing too.

'Silence!' bellowed Black Texta. 'Since we're all here, I now call this meeting to order.'

'Not another meeting!' groaned Jade. 'Things worked just fine without meetings until the textas moved in. We fell into line when Ralph opened the pencil-case, drew or wrote what Ralph wanted, and then went back in

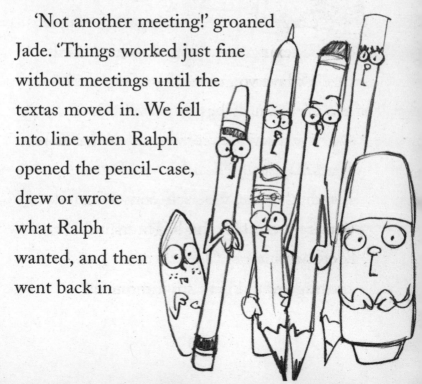

again when he was finished. Easy. There's
no need for these silly meetings …'

A mean-looking rubber with narrow slits
for eyes barked ferociously at Jade,
silencing her. Black Texta gave her a stern
look and went on with the meeting.

'As most of you
know, the summer
holidays are over
and school starts
tomorrow. Ralph
will be taking us to school in his pencil-
case every day, and taking us out during
lessons when he has to write or draw. Since
we have a few newcomers …' at that point
Black Texta stared directly at Penny,
making her feel very self-conscious indeed,
'I will go through the Rules again.

'Rule Number One: all talking and
moving around is to stop immediately

when Ralph opens the zip, and for the whole time the zip is left open.

'Rule Number Two: no biro, pencil, crayon, texta, permanent marker or highlighter is to write or draw on anything, unless propelled by Ralph's hand. This includes correcting colouring-in outside the lines and correcting spelling mistakes. Ralph can make such corrections himself with the help of Rubber,' Black Texta nodded his head towards the mean-looking rubber, 'or, in extreme cases,' continued Black Texta, shuddering a little, 'Gloop.'

All the writing implements looked over to where a dirty bottle of correction fluid was cowering by himself in the corner. He had spilled a lot of his insides all down his front, and his label was barely readable. Penny got the feeling that the other writing implements didn't like him very much.

'Rule Number Three:' continued Black Texta, 'anyone who breaks these rules will be instantly expelled from the pencil-case!'

A murmur of fright went around all the writing implements. Only Black Texta and Rubber were quiet, looking sternly around at the others. Gloop started to quiver so badly that he leaked even more of his insides all over his label. Penny hopped over to Gloop to see if she could help.

'Stay away,' whispered Gloop. 'If they see you talking to me, nobody else will be friends with you!' and he turned away from Penny before she could even open her mouth.

'Now,' boomed Black Texta's loud voice. 'Everyone is to go to sleep. The first day of school is a big day, and we all have to be in top form for when Ralph wants to write with us!'

Penny noticed that all the other writing implements were trying to move as far away from Gloop as possible. She felt sorry for him, so lay down as close to him as she dared, without making the others think she was being friends with him. She missed Dictionary. In the shop, she and Dictionary had spent hours talking to each other and spelling words once it got dark. She pulled her sticky-tape around her for warmth and went to sleep to the sound of Gloop's quiet sobbing.

chapter 3

First Day of School

When Penny woke up, she couldn't believe
it was morning. Normally she would hear
the sounds of Mr McPaper opening the
blinds and sunlight would fill the shop.
This morning everything was still dark.
Then suddenly all the walls seemed to cave
in around Penny, and pencils, textas and
crayons all crowded in on top of her.

'Ralph! Have you packed your school
bag?' called a voice from outside the pencil-
case, that sounded very much like Ralph's
mother's.

'Yes! I'm just getting my pencil-case!'

There was a loud bang, then all the
pencils and crayons that had been
squashing Penny the instant before rolled
away from her again.

'What was that?' Penny asked, in spite of
herself. In the dark she could just make out
the shape of Gloop. In the crush of writing
implements, she must have been pushed
towards him.

'Just Ralph putting us in his school bag,' whispered Gloop. 'Now quickly, roll away from me again before anyone sees you!'

Penny did as she was told. Gloop seemed friendlier than all the other implements in the pencil-case – at least he would talk to her! Penny would have liked to talk to him longer, but he had already turned around and was facing the wall again.

The trip to school wasn't much fun. It was bumpy, and textas, pencils and crayons kept rolling into Penny. At one point she found herself pushed right up against the side of the pencil-case. Whatever the pencil-case was next to was very cold. Penny pulled her sticky-tape around her tightly for warmth.

24

'That'll be Ralph's frozen drink. His mother always packs him one on the first day of school,' whispered Gloop, noticing Penny's chattering teeth.

After a while Penny managed to warm up and noticed that the pencil-case had stopped moving. All the other implements in the pencil-case were lining up in neat rows. Penny hopped into line behind a pink crayon, and just in time, as Black Texta and Rubber were walking up and down the rows, making sure nobody was talking.

'First lesson is about to begin,' said Black Texta, his voice a little quieter than last night, but still just as headmaster-like. 'Remember the Rules, and no talking!' he said, kicking the short green pencil that had been whispering during the meeting the night before.

Just as Black Texta finished speaking

there was a loud zipping sound, and light flooded the pencil-case for the first time that morning. Penny saw a hand reach into the pencil-case and push writing implements from side to side. She tried to sink lower into the pencil-case to get away from the hand. The fingers closed around a bunch of coloured pencils and then both the hand and the pencils disappeared from the pencil-case, leaving a big gap. Penny breathed a big sigh of relief and rolled into the middle of the gap. She blinked twice, and when she opened her eyes the second time the hand had returned! The hand came closer and closer, then Penny felt the thumb and two fingers close around her, and suddenly she was lifted into the air!

'Wow! That looks just like my new pencil!' Penny heard a familiar girl's voice say, but she couldn't see who it was because

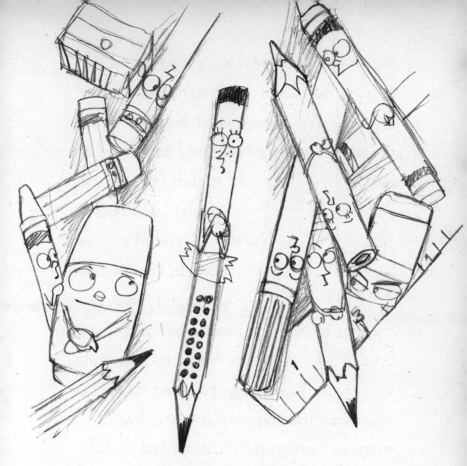

the bright sunlight was making her squint.

'Got it free with my dictionary!' said a
voice Penny recognised as Ralph's. Penny
squinted up along the arm that was holding
her, and saw that it was attached to Ralph's
body. She smiled up at him, but he was

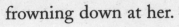

frowning down at her.
'What's the matter?'
asked the girl.
'My hand keeps
sticking to this stupid
pencil,' said Ralph.
'Give it here,' said
the girl. Penny felt a
new hand close
around her and snatch
her out of Ralph's hand.
The girl tugged sharply at
Penny's sticky-tape. Penny heard a
rrrrrrrrrrrrrrrip and suddenly her middle
felt very cold.

'There you go,' said the girl, passing
Penny back to Ralph and rolling the sticky-
tape she had just torn off Penny into a little
ball.

'Thanks, Sarah,' said Ralph, gripping

Penny tightly. 'That feels much better!'

And before Penny knew what was happening, Ralph was pressing her toe against some paper and dragging her around on it.

Penny looked down and noticed that she was leaving a black trail behind on the page. She looked up at Ralph who was frowning in concentration, the tip of his tongue poking out the side of his mouth.

Penny looked at where Ralph was guiding her and saw that the end of the paper was getting close. If Ralph didn't stop soon, she was going to make a big, black mark all over the table!

At the very last second, Ralph lifted Penny off the paper and carried her all the way back to the other side.

But Ralph didn't go exactly back to where he'd started. There was a blue line between the first black trail that Penny had left on the paper and the new trail that her toe was making. Penny looked closely at the first trail, and suddenly realised that the shape of the black trail was familiar. It was a line of words! Penny was writing!

Penny looked at the words proudly until she noticed some of them were spelled incorrectly. That would never do! Whatever would Dictionary say?

Penny quickly looked down at the new word Ralph was writing: 'BUDGET". But Ralph had forgotten the 'D'! Penny kicked hard with her toe to make Ralph write a 'D' and the word was spelled correctly. As Ralph guided her along the paper, Penny kicked and hopped and shimmied and skated to help Ralph spell all the words correctly. Finally, Ralph put an exhausted Penny down and took his piece of paper up to the teacher's desk at the front of the classroom.

'Well done, Ralph!' said Mrs Sword, the teacher. 'Only two spelling mistakes in the first line, and the rest is perfect. You should be very proud of yourself!'

When Ralph got back to his seat he was blushing with pride, and there was a big gold star at the bottom of the page, with the word 'Excellent' next to it, written in

green ink. Penny was feeling quite proud of
herself too.

Finally the bell rang and Ralph put
Penny and the coloured pencils back in the
pencil-case. They were all chatting excitedly

about their first lesson at school when all of a sudden the chattering stopped and a big, black shadow fell over Penny. Penny turned around slowly. Black Texta was standing right in front of her, with a very nasty look on his face. Rubber was standing next to him, baring his teeth and growling at Penny.

'Ms Penny Pencil,' began Black Texta in his loud voice.

'Y-y-yes?' said Penny, feeling even smaller than she had the night before.

'I have it on good authority that Ralph got an "Excellent" for his spelling this morning. Is that correct?'

'Yes,' said Penny brightening, wondering why Black Texta was acting as though this was a bad thing.

'And you were the pencil he was using?' sneered Black Texta.

'Yes, I was!' said Penny quite proudly.

'Did you help him spell any words at all?' asked Black Texta, in an almost friendly voice.

'Well, I gave a little kick here and there ...' began Penny modestly. To the left of Black Texta Penny could see Gloop shaking his head urgently.

'Have you forgotten Rule Number Two!' bellowed Black Texta, so loudly that all the other writing implements huddled closely together in fright.

Penny didn't know what to say. She was so scared and exhausted that she couldn't even remember Rule Number One. 'What's Rule Number Two?' she asked, in a very small voice.

'No biro, pencil, crayon, texta, permanent marker or highlighter is to write or draw on anything, unless propelled by Ralph's hand. This includes correcting colouring-in

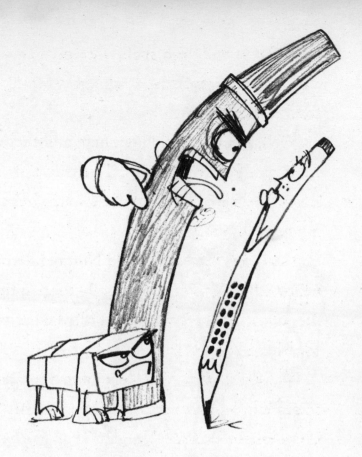

outside the lines and … correcting spelling
mistakes!' boomed Black Texta.

Penny felt herself start to shake. All the
other implements were quivering a little
too.

'And what,' began Black Texta, turning

around and kicking the old pink crayon Penny had stood next to in line that morning, 'is Rule Number Three?'

'Anyone who breaks these rules will be instantly expelled from the pencil-case,' murmured the crayon sadly, not daring to look either Black Texta or Penny in the eye.

Penny suddenly realised that she had broken the pencil-case rules and was going to be expelled! Black Texta sneered down at her, as Rubber made his way towards the zip to force it open from the inside.

'Wait!' said a voice Penny barely recognised. It was Gloop. Penny had only ever heard him whisper before, but his voice now was loud and clear.

Black Texta whirled around on his heel. 'Was that you, Gloop?' he said, his eyes narrowing and his mouth curling into a sneer.

'Yes,' said Gloop, seeming a lot braver than he had the night before. 'She's only new, and she had a big day yesterday. You can't expect her to do everything perfectly her first day on the job. After all, we all make mistakes,' said Gloop pointedly.

Penny wasn't sure, but she thought she saw Black Texta make the tiniest of flinches. None of the other writing implements seemed to notice – they were all scowling at Gloop with distaste.

'Fine!' boomed Black Texta, then whirled back around to face Penny. 'We'll let you off this time, missy. But if you, or anyone else,' he shouted, glaring around the pencil-case, 'ever breaks another Rule, it will be instant expulsion!'

chapter 4

The Good Old Days

Penny spent the next few days trying to
keep as far away from Black Texta as
possible. None of the other writing
implements wanted anything to do with
her, and Penny wondered if being expelled
would have actually been worse than the
way she was now being treated. Even
Gloop wouldn't talk to her at first, but once
he realised that none of the other writing
implements were being nice to her either,
he stopped pretending not to like her, and
they became great friends.

One night, after all the pencils had gone

to sleep – apart from the orange and green ones which were always up late gossiping – Gloop told Penny all about the good old days in the pencil-case.

'Everything was wonderful before the textas moved in. Pencils played with crayons, everyone was friends. Then the textas arrived. Tall and shiny – they thought they were better than the pencils

and crayons because they had caps,' said Gloop, snorting.

'Very proud of their caps, they were,' continued Gloop. 'Made them a

good deal taller than everyone else. And
when the textas took their caps off, there
was the strangest of smells. Made a few of
the pencils feel all
woozey! They started
colouring in outside the
lines and all manner
of things!'

Penny snuck a peak at Black Texta, who
was fast asleep and snoring loudly. He lay
between the textas and the other
implements, making a natural barrier that
none of the others dared cross. Black
Texta's casing was moving up and down in
time with his snoring, and his cap was
rammed on tightly. Rubber was sleeping
only millimetres away from Black Texta's
cap. Penny knew if anyone rolled too close

to Black Texta, Rubber would wake up instantly and attack. In spite of herself, Penny shuddered.

'The textas had much stronger colours than the pencils, and before long, Ralph was using them all the time. Even though sometimes Ralph would press too hard with a texta and it would stain the paper through to the other side, he still preferred to use textas for colouring-in. The coloured pencils didn't like this, of course, but there was nothing they could do about it. They tried jostling with the textas to get closer to the zip whenever Ralph opened the pencil-case, but any time Ralph picked them up, it was only to get them out of the way so he could get to the textas more easily.'

Penny remembered hiding in the bottom of the pencil-case the first time Ralph's hand had entered it, fishing around for her.

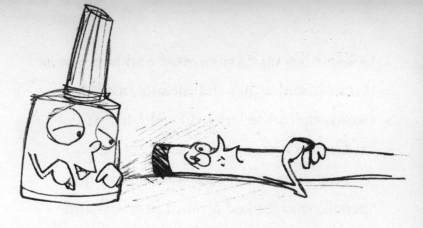

'Is that why nobody likes me very much?'
she said in a small voice, 'because Ralph
likes to write with me?'

Gloop looked at her kindly, but didn't
answer her question.

'The textas certainly were the writing
implements of choice in those days,'
continued Gloop, 'and for a short time
things were going well. The pencils were
actually much happier. Although they
didn't get to draw and colour in as much,
they soon realised that they didn't need to
be sharpened quite so often either.'

'Sharpened?' said Penny, wondering what

sharpening was. Dictionary had only got as far as teaching her the meanings of all the words up to the letter 'Q'. She hadn't got around to learning 'S' yet.

Her voice seemed to wake up a yellow pencil, who looked around in fright and tried to burrow into the bundle of blue and red pencils nearby.

Gloop looked at Penny sternly.

'Sorry,' she mumbled, 'but what's …
sharpening?' she asked in a whisper.

'Sharpening is what happens to pencils when they get blunt.'

Penny knew what blunt meant. It was when a pencil couldn't write any more.

'But isn't sharpening a good thing?' she asked. 'The pencils can write better afterwards, right? I'm looking forward to my first sharpening!'

Gloop frowned and shook his head.

'Sharpening might be a good thing for pencils,' he began, 'but it's very painful.'

'Oh,' said Penny, not looking forward to her first sharpening quite so much any more. 'How does it happen?'

'Well,' said Gloop, 'the blunt end of the pencil goes into the sharpener, and gets twisted around.'

'What does the sharpener do?' asked

Penny, her curiosity making her voice a little louder. All around her, sleeping pencils huddled in closer together.

Gloop frowned at her again.

'Sorry!' she whispered.

'The sharpener scrapes off the wood on the outside of the pencil and files the lead down to a fine point. It's very painful,' whispered Gloop, 'and the pencils always come out of the sharpener a few millimetres shorter!'

Penny finally understood why the coloured pencils were all different heights.

'When will *I* need sharpening?' she asked very quietly.

'If Ralph keeps writing with you as much as he has been, you'll need sharpening very soon,' said Gloop, avoiding Penny's eye and pretending to be very interested in an ink stain on the wall of the pencil-case.

'Oh,' said Penny, feeling nervous. 'And what about the textas? They're all the same size. Do they need to be sharpened?'

'No,' he said finally. 'They're made of ink and plastic. They'll never need sharpening.'

'Why does Black Texta hate me so much?' asked Penny.

Gloop shook his head sadly. 'I don't know. The textas don't seem to like anyone who's not a texta. Real snobs. But,' said Gloop yawning, 'it's getting very late, and you've got a big day of writing ahead of you tomorrow. You'd better go to sleep.'

And with that Gloop rolled over and faced away from Penny. Penny was sure there was a lot more that he wasn't telling her. Her mind was absolutely buzzing with unanswered questions and it took her a long time to get to sleep.

When Gloop finally heard Penny's tiny

little snores, he quietly rolled a little closer
to her to make sure she stayed safe and
warm.

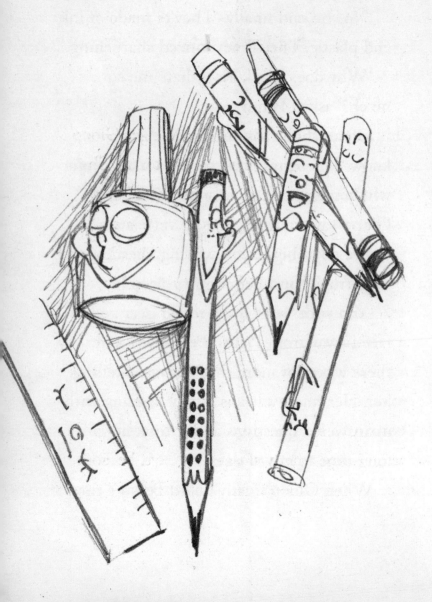

chapter 5

A Clever Idea

Try as she might, Penny couldn't get Gloop
to say anything more about the textas. She
asked him a number of times, but Gloop
would always change the subject. On
Gloop's part, he managed to distract Penny
by coming up with a very clever plan to
teach Ralph how to spell.

One day Ralph left Gloop, Penny and
Dictionary on his desk, while he took his
exercise book up to Mrs Sword's desk to be
corrected. Ralph had taken to zipping his
pencil-case tightly shut these days, because
a nasty boy called Bert who sat behind

Ralph and Sarah had an equally nasty habit
of pushing their pencil-cases off the desk
when they weren't looking, so that the
contents spilled all over the floor. Although
Penny, Gloop and Dictionary still had to
keep an eye out for their own safety,
Dictionary used Ralph's absence as an
opportunity to have stern words with Penny.

'I can't believe I spent the whole summer
teaching you how to spell if you're going to
let him hand in rubbish like that!' he scolded.

'I've already told you,' shouted Penny in frustration, 'I'm not allowed to help! I'll get expelled from the pencil-case forever. You know what Black Texta's like!' Poor Penny was close to tears. It broke her heart to have to misspell words, but she was banned from correcting Ralph's spelling.

When Bert got up to take his own work up to Mrs Sword's desk, he bumped the desk accidentally-on-purpose, making Ralph's pencil-case fall on the floor. Gloop took the opportunity to roll over to where Dictionary and Penny were having their argument.

'Could I make a suggestion?' said Gloop, getting to his feet.

'Yes?' said Dictionary scornfully. He was a little bit jealous of Penny's new friend

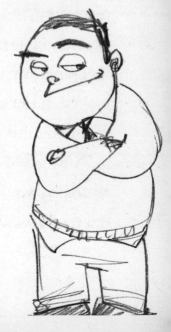

and was against the idea of correction fluid on principle. Words should be spelled correctly the first time, not simply painted over if the person writing them doesn't know how to spell!

'Maybe we could all work together and teach Ralph to spell, rather than just correct his mistakes,' said Gloop.

'Fantastic!' said Dictionary sarcastically. 'Just what his parents and teachers have been trying to do for years! And how, exactly, Mr Gloop, do you propose we teach him to spell, where trained human professionals have failed?'

'Here's my plan,' began Gloop. He moved closer to Dictionary and Penny and whispered his idea.

'Now go back to your desk and look up all the words I've underlined in green in the dictionary, and don't come back until they're all spelled correctly!' boomed Mrs Sword's loud voice from the front of the classroom.

Moments later, Ralph flopped back into his chair. He picked his pencil-case up off the floor and pulled out Rubber. Ralph started angrily rubbing out all the words underlined in green by Mrs Sword's pen. Every time Rubber came anywhere near Penny, he snapped at her with his big teeth.

Once Ralph had erased all the misspelled words, he put Rubber back in the pencil-case and picked up Penny again. As always, Rubber had accidentally-on-purpose left little shavings all over the paper. Normally this annoyed Penny, because it was very difficult for her to write over the shavings. But today she was pleased that the shavings were there. She managed a quick little wink to let Gloop and Dictionary know that part one of the plan was working.

The next time Ralph started to misspell a word, Penny allowed herself to get stuck on a rubber shaving and stop writing. She refused to start writing again until Ralph had used Dictionary to look up the word and spell it correctly. Every other time Ralph tried to misspell a word, Penny would trip over a rubber shaving and stop writing, forcing Ralph to look up the word in Dictionary. By the time Ralph had finished, both Penny and Dictionary were exhausted. Ralph took his work back up to Mrs Sword's desk just before the bell rang.

'I'll correct this overnight, and give it back to you in the morning,' said Mrs Sword. 'And for goodness sake, don't forget to study for your sums test tomorrow! Class dismissed.'

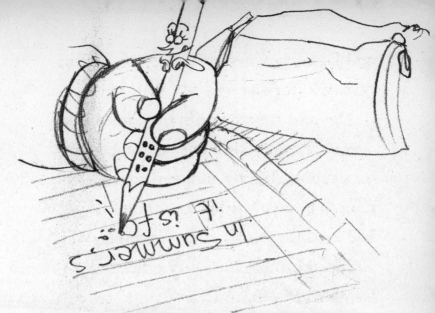

Ralph stuffed Penny and Gloop back
into the pencil-case, and put the rest of his
belongings into his school bag. He had
forgotten all about the sums test. Next to
spelling, sums was his worst subject. There
was no way he was going to pass the sums
test tomorrow.

Sarah was waiting for him just outside
the classroom door.

'I thought you weren't coming. I was just
about to go back in and get you!' she said.

Ralph just grunted and looked at his shoes.

'Granny wants to know if you want to come over and play this afternoon. She said she's making your favourite cake ...' said Sarah, trying to cheer Ralph up.

'Thanks,' said Ralph, 'but I really need to study for the sums test tomorrow.'

'I could help you ...' suggested Sarah.

'Look! I don't need help, all right? Just because I'm no good at sums doesn't mean you have to feel sorry for me ...' said Ralph quite angrily.

'Fine!' said Sarah, just as angrily. 'I was just trying to be nice, that's all! If you want to fail your sums test, I don't care!' And she ran off around the corner without looking back.

Ralph felt terrible. He hadn't meant to upset Sarah, but she shouldn't have rubbed his nose in it for being rubbish at sums. Once he got home, he went straight to his room and spent the rest of the evening practising long division. But no matter how hard he concentrated, the answer he got never matched the answer in the back of the book.

Ralph's mother came into his bedroom at half past nine to say goodnight. She was surprised to see him still sitting at his desk doing his homework.

'Ralph! It's half past nine!' she said. 'You should be in bed!'

'I don't feel well,' said Ralph, which wasn't a lie at all, because he had a very bad feeling in his stomach whenever he thought of the sums test. 'Maybe I should stay home from school tomorrow?' he suggested hopefully.

Ralph's mother looked at the sums books on the desk, and the piles of paper that were scattered on the floor with big crosses all over them.

'Sums study not going so well?' she asked kindly.

'It's awful! I hate sums. I'm going to fail tomorrow!' said Ralph in despair.

'Oh, Ralph,' said his mother, helping him into his pyjamas. 'You're just tired now.

Things will be better in the morning, I
promise. Now go to sleep,' she said, tucking
him in and turning the light off.

Both Ralph and his mother had
forgotten to close the sums book, which
Penny was lying on top of. There was just
enough moonlight coming in through the
crack in the curtains for Penny to see. She
began to read.

The Sums Test

Ralph was not in a good mood the next morning. He hadn't slept very well, and he noticed dark circles under his eyes in the mirror while he was brushing his teeth. When he knocked on Sarah's door on the

way to school, her grandmother answered and said that Sarah had already left. When Ralph finally caught up with Sarah at school she refused to talk to him. She even told him to shut up when he tried to apologise!

'Ooo-oooh,' said Bert, the nasty boy who sat behind Ralph and Sarah when he realised the two were fighting. 'What's wrong, your girlfriend wouldn't kiss you, Ralph-eee?'

'She's not my girlfriend,' said Ralph through clenched teeth.

'Course she isn't! You're too ugly!' said Bert.

That was too much for Ralph. Sitting in front of Bert on a good day was bad enough, but today, when he was about to fail his sums test, and his best friend wouldn't talk to him, being teased by Bert was the last thing Ralph needed. He whirled around and punched Bert on the nose as hard as he could. In fact, Ralph hit Bert so hard that Bert fell over backwards in his chair and his nose started bleeding. Then something happened that none of the children in the classroom had ever seen before. Bert began to cry. Ralph looked at Sarah, who was staring at him with her mouth wide open in surprise.

'What's going on here?' said a loud voice.

Ralph turned around to see Mrs Sword standing right behind him! His hand was still clenched in a fist, which Mrs Sword noticed.

'Did you punch Bert, Ralph?'

Ralph nodded. He was still so stunned that he had actually punched Bert hard enough to make him cry that he was lost for words.

'Headmaster's office right now,' said Mrs
Sword. 'And take this with you. No point
wasting time while you're waiting outside
in the corridor.'

Ralph looked at the piece of paper Mrs
Sword had given him. It was the sums test.
His mood, which had improved remarkably
since he'd punched Bert, sunk straight back

down again.

'Just take a pencil with you,' said Mrs Sword. 'And no rubber.'

Penny wriggled her way to the top of the pencil-case so that Ralph would be able to pull her out easily. Then off they went to the headmaster's office.

But Ralph didn't start his sums test straight away. He paced up and down the corridor for quite a few minutes until he calmed down. Finally he started the test paper.

Penny noticed that Ralph
wasn't holding her quite
the way she was used to.
She had a quick peek
at the back of his
hand. The
knuckles were
bleeding a
little from
where he had
punched Bert. As
Ralph made a mistake
in the first sum, Penny gave
the smallest of kicks and Ralph's hand
moved obligingly to write the correct
number on the paper.

'This will be easier than I thought!' said
Penny. With none of the other writing
implements around, and Ralph's hand
being weaker than usual, she was able to

make him write all the right answers with only a minimum of effort!

When the headmaster called Ralph into his office, Ralph stuffed Penny into his back pocket. Penny couldn't hear anything at all in the back pocket, which disappointed all the other pencils and textas when she finally got back to the pencil-case because they all wanted a full report of what had gone on in the headmaster's office. Even though Penny didn't have anything to tell them, they all thought she was quite the hero. Even Black Texta didn't come out with any of his usual nasty comments, but he and Rubber still wore dirty looks on their faces.

Ralph's school mates thought of him as quite a hero too. None of them had ever dared to say anything back to Bert when he teased them, much less punch him in the nose and make him cry!

Sarah seemed to have completely forgotten all about their fight the day before and said she was sure her grandmother would still have some cake left if Ralph wanted to come over and play that afternoon.

Even Mrs Sword seemed to forget that little boys aren't supposed to punch each other. When she handed the sums tests back, she proudly announced that Ralph had come top of the class.

Ralph's mother was so pleased with the results of his sums test that when he came back from playing at Sarah's she let him do his homework on the sofa, while watching TV! All in all, things were going very well for Ralph and Penny indeed.

When Ralph's mother called him to the table for dinner, Black Texta called all the

writing implements together for an
important assembly. Penny and all the
pencils and crayons were quite excited.
They thought maybe Black Texta was
going to say something nice about Penny
for a change. Only Gloop was uneasy. He
didn't like the way Black Texta and Rubber
were looking at Penny, or the way that the
other textas were slowly surrounding her.
He tried to move closer to Penny to protect

her, but he found he couldn't move. A big, fat permanent marker with the word 'Fright' in white writing down its side was blocking his way.

'Outta my way!' said Gloop loudly, but the other pencils and crayons were chattering so loudly and excitedly that nobody heard him.

'You won't be going anywhere,' said the Fright permanent marker, nastily.

Gloop tried to dodge around him, but the Fright permanent marker just laughed at him.

'There's nothing you can do to save her now, Gloop,' said the marker menacingly.

Gloop struggled to get away from him, but as the marker unscrewed his cap he knew it was too late. A very strong inky smell came out of

the Fright permanent marker and poor
Gloop fell unconscious.

'I call this assembly to order,' boomed
Black Texta.

Silence fell over the pencils and crayons.
Penny looked around for Gloop, but all she
could see were textas. She started to feel a
little uneasy, although all the pencils and
crayons seemed relaxed and happy.

'As you know, Ralph had a most
extraordinary day today,' began Black
Texta. The pencils and crayons applauded
Ralph, even though he wasn't there to hear
them. 'He punched Bert in the nose, got
sent to the headmaster's office, got top
marks for his sums test, and was even
allowed to do his homework while
watching TV!'

'The way Black Texta's talking about it,
you'd think he was personally responsible

for it all!' whispered Jade the short green pencil to her tall, orange friend Amber.

'Of course, Ralph didn't achieve this all on his own,' continued Black Texta.

'Here he goes, going to take some of the credit for himself,' muttered Amber.

'Someone in this pencil-case helped him. And we all know who that someone is, don't we?' said Black Texta, smiling in a way that Penny didn't quite trust. 'That someone is Penny!'

At that, all the pencils and crayons applauded, but Penny felt very uneasy as they all turned to look at her, and the other textas started to close in.

'Tell us, Penny, how exactly did Ralph manage to get all the answers right on his sums test?'

Penny's throat went dry.

'Did you maybe help him a little, while

he was waiting outside the headmaster's office?'

Penny knew it was no use lying, but she didn't want to give Black Texta the satisfaction of hearing her confess. She stood firmly, and didn't say a word.

'Cat got your tongue?' hissed Black Texta.

All the pencils and crayons looked from Black Texta to Penny and back again, as though they were watching a tennis match. The merry mood of moments ago had completely disappeared.

'Where's Gloop?' thought Penny, knowing that it was going to take a miracle to save her this time. But unknown to Penny, Gloop was still unconscious, being held prisoner by the Fright permanent marker.

'Well, if you're not going to say anything,' said Black Texta threateningly, 'maybe our guest will!'

Black Texta stepped aside, and all the writing implements fell silent. They were looking at the only writing implement on earth more frightening than Black Texta – Mrs Sword's Green Pen!

Penny didn't think Mrs Sword's Green Pen looked all that frightening, but when the pen spoke, her voice cut straight through to Penny's soul.

'Penny, I could tell you had been manipulating Ralph's hand. His handwriting looked quite different to normal, but exactly the same as when you tried to correct his spelling mistakes on the first day of school. You might have been able to fool Ralph and his teacher into thinking that he

73

can do sums, but you should know by now that the pen is mightier than Mrs Sword!'

All the other pencils and crayons shuffled their feet uneasily. Penny's heart was beating quickly. She couldn't decide who she loathed more: Black Texta or Mrs Sword's Green Pen.

'I believe this isn't her first offence,' continued the hateful Green Pen.

'No,' said Black Texta. 'Gloop managed to argue her case for her the last time. I can't think why he isn't jumping to her defence now, the rotten little coward,' he continued, in a tone of voice that made Penny realise he knew exactly where Gloop was, and that something very horrible must have happened to him.

'In that case, an expulsion is definitely in order,' said Mrs Sword's Green Pen.

'I don't think a simple expulsion is

enough,' said Black Texta menacingly. Penny glared at Black Texta through narrowed eyes. Being expelled and away from Black Texta for good really didn't worry her, although she was quite anxious to find Gloop and make sure he was all right.

'Probably not,' agreed Mrs Sword's Green Pen, consulting what looked like a very big, old rule book that had appeared out of nowhere. 'The appropriate punishment for this sort of offence ... is ... sharpening.'

At the mention of the word, even the textas that had been drawing in around Penny seemed to catch their breath in fright.

'She's looking a little blunt as it is,' said Mrs Sword's Green Pen, peering over the top of her glasses at Penny.

'Oh, no,' breathed Penny, starting to tremble.

She turned to run, but the textas that were surrounding her closed in even more tightly. She looked wildly from one side of the circle to the other. A gap appeared between a purple and yellow texta. Penny started to run towards it, when suddenly Rubber, Black Texta and Mrs Sword's Green Pen walked through it.

The green and dark blue texta standing behind Penny grabbed her very tightly. Rubber paced over to her, dragging a shiny object with him … the sharpener! Penny had never seen it before. It had two holes, one was very small, but the other one was just the right size for Penny's foot. Penny tried to pull away from the textas, but they held her fast as Rubber forced the sharpener onto her toe and slowly turned it.

Penny had never felt such pain before in her life. It felt like her whole foot was being sliced off. And to her horror, she saw bits of her foot appearing on the outside of the sharpener!

'That's enough. I'll take it from here,' said Black Texta, grabbing Penny from the textas and yanking her out of the sharpener. Penny's foot felt better instantly, and to her delight her toe was nice and pointy again, instead of being all round and blunt. Penny was so busy admiring her toe, she didn't notice what was happening until she heard a zzzzzzzzzzzipping sound and realised Black Texta was pushing her towards the open zipper.

The other pencils and crayons gathered around, looking frightened and sorry for Penny. Penny tried to look past them, to see if she could spot Gloop, but he was nowhere to be seen.

'What have you done with Gloop?' she

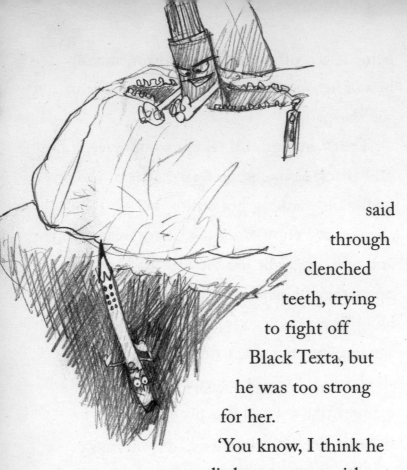

said
through
clenched
teeth, trying
to fight off
Black Texta, but
he was too strong
for her.

'You know, I think he
was a little overcome with
Fright!' said Black Texta, giving her a final
shove out the zipper.

As Penny fell, all she could hear was the
sound of Black Texta's laughter, then she
was totally enveloped in blackness.

chapter 7

Under the Cushions

The first thing Penny became aware of was intense pain all along her body, and strange hissing noises in her head.

'What'ssss that?'

'Issss it a casssst-out like ussss?'

'It lookssss like it'ssss a pencsssil.'

'Hassss it been exsssspelled from itssss pencsssssil casssse?'

Penny lifted her head and shook it. As she opened her eyes, she realised that the noises were not coming from inside her head, but from the strange creatures that were surrounding her.

'Look! It'ssss moving!' said one of the creatures.

'Doessss it have a name?' said another.

'Maybe it doessssn't ssspeak Englisssh,' said a third.

'Of course I speak Englissssh!' said Penny huffily. 'And don't call me "it". My name'ssss Penny,' she continued angrily, imitating the way the strange creatures spoke. 'Who are you?'

The creatures all looked at each other, then the first one spoke: 'We ussssed to be important. But now we're usssselessss piecsssesssss of rubbisssh living behind the cussssshionssss on the ssssofa.'

'How long have you been here?' asked Penny.

'We're not ssssure, maybe dayssss, maybe monthssss, maybe longer,' said the second creature.

'It'ssss hard to tell in the darknessss,' said
the third.

Something suddenly occurred to Penny.

'Has anyone else arrived recently?'

'Recssssently?' said the first creature.

'You see, I'm looking for my friend
Gloop …'

'Gloop? What'ssss Gloop?' interrupted the second creature.

'He's. My. Friend,' said Penny, barely managing to control her temper. 'And he's in terrible danger.'

'Gloop'ssss in danger,' said the third creature.

'Look, why do you all talk so strangely?' asked Penny. Her head ached and she was getting fed up with the silly creatures. Plus, she was very worried about what had happened to Gloop.

'I dunno,' said the first creature, without hissing. 'Passes the time, I s'pose.'

'But we haven't got any time to lose! They've got Gloop, and we have to save him!' said Penny urgently.

'Who has Gloop?' asked the second creature, also speaking normally.

'The textas!' exploded Penny.

'You don't mean the textas in Ralph's pencil-case, do you?' asked the third creature.

'As a matter of fact, I do!' said Penny, hopeful that now the creatures knew the seriousness of the situation they would help.

The three creatures fell silent. Penny glared at them.

'Well? Are you going to help me save him?' asked Penny, trying to climb out from between the cushions. But the harder she tried to climb up, the further down she seemed to sink.

'I wouldn't bother,' said the first creature. 'You'll never get out. Once you're lost behind the cushions, there's no escape.'

Penny decided to ignore him and kept trying to climb up the cushions. But it was no use. She was stuck.

'Glooooooooooooooop …' she called.

'He can't hear you,' said the second creature. 'When you're behind the cushions, you're gone for good. Not even your voice can escape.'

'But the textas have got him …'

'We know,' said the third creature. 'THEN WHY WON'T YOU HELP ME DO SOMETHING ABOUT IT?' shouted Penny.

'Forget it,' said the third creature. 'They're nasty pieces of work. If they've got your friend, there's no way of saving him. I s'pose that big black texta is the one responsible for chucking you out then. Or maybe the rubber. Never liked either of them much.'

Penny looked hard at the third creature. It was difficult to make out shapes in the gloom, but he looked round, thin, and quite short, with a pointy head.

'What are you?' said Penny, straining to

see in the dark. 'And how do you know so much about what goes on in the pencil-case?'

The third creature beckoned to the other two, who wandered over to him. They were all the same thickness and had stripes that were all the same colour. The second one climbed onto the first one, and the third one clambered on top of them both. Then Penny saw: all three of them together made a single pencil!

'What happened to you?' asked Penny, astonished to see that the three creatures had originally been parts of the same pencil.

'The textas,' said the first creature, who

was the bottom of the pencil. 'They think ink is better than lead. They moved in, took one look at me – I mean us – and decided it was time to go. By the way, I'm Stubbs, this is Umbilica, and the short guy up the top is Lead.'

'They started an exercise they called "ethnink cleansing" to get rid of all the grey lead pencils,' said Umbilica from the middle of the pencil. 'They made up silly rules that we couldn't possibly obey, and then used that as an excuse to expel us from the pencil-case.'

'Unfortunately, when they pushed us out, we landed on something really hard, and broke into three pieces,' said Lead, from the top of the pencil.

'What did you land on?' asked Penny curiously.

There was a loud rumble and the whole

sofa began to shake so
violently that Umbilica
and Lead fell off
Stubbs and all three
tumbled onto the
cushions below. Penny
squinted and saw a
large, black creature
with coloured buttons
on its belly rise up
behind the shards of
pencil.

'They landed on
me,' it said.

'Did you used to
live in the pencil-case
too?' Penny asked the
stranger.

'Did I ... used to
...' chuckled the

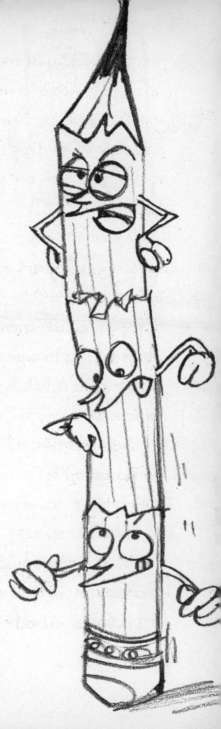

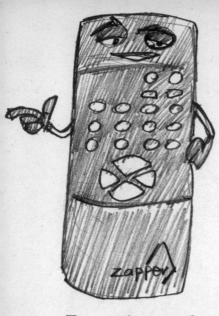

stranger. 'I should think not! Don't you know what I am?' he laughed.

'Erm, no,' said Penny.

'I'm a TV remote control!' said the stranger. 'My name's Zapper, but my friends call me Frank. I don't belong in a pencil-case!' he chuckled again. 'I don't belong behind the cushions either,' he admitted as an afterthought.

'No one belongs behind the cushions!' said Lead. 'You just end up here by accident and kind of get stuck.'

'That's true,' said Zapper. 'But it was fun at first. People would sit on the sofa and I'd change the channel when they were least expecting it. Always got a bit of a laugh.

Until my batteries went flat, that is …'

'But what about Gloop?' said Penny, suddenly remembering her friend was in danger.

'I'm afraid that unless Gloop also gets chucked out of the pencil-case,' began Umbilica, 'and ends up behind – WHAT ON EARTH ARE YOU DOING?' she screamed.

'What do you mean?' asked Penny, looking around in alarm.

'YOU'RE BLEEDING ALL OVER THE SOFA!' yelled Umbilica.

'I'm what? Oh no!' said Penny. She looked down at her toe and saw that the tip had snapped off, leaving behind a big, black mark on the cushion. Penny tried to brush the mark off the cushion but only

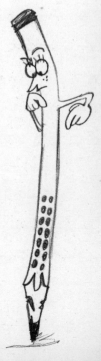

succeeded in grinding it into the white fabric.

'Don't worry,' said Stubbs. 'If people can't find a pencil or a TV remote control, they're hardly going to notice a little black mark.'

'Hmmm,' said Penny quietly, thinking if she made the mark big enough, she and the other exiles might get noticed. All she'd have to do was wait until the others were distracted, then subtly wiggle her toe around to make the stain bigger. Penny smiled to herself and rejoined the conversation.

chapter 8

The Big, Black Mark

A few days later Ralph was in his room doing his homework in red pencil. He'd lost Penny a few days ago, and although he and Sarah had looked everywhere at school and at both their houses, they hadn't been able to find her. Ralph jumped when he heard his mother yelling from the living-room:

'Ralph! How many times have I told you to put your pens and pencils away when you're finished with them?'

'About five hundred,' mumbled Ralph, as he slowly walked into the living-room to see what all the fuss was about.

'Something has put a big black mark all over the cushion! Look!' said his mother angrily, hurling the offending cushion at him.

Ralph caught the cushion easily – his mother hadn't really thrown it that hard – and looked at the tell-tale stain.

'I'm sorry, Mum. It was an accident,' said Ralph.

His mother looked at him with one eyebrow raised.

'It doesn't really matter though, does it?' said Ralph. 'We're having the new sofa delivered tomorrow, aren't we?'

'That's not the point!' said his mother. 'I promised Sarah's grandmother that they could have the old sofa. I couldn't believe how uncomfortable theirs was the other afternoon when I went around there to pick you up. I can't possibly give them this sofa now with such a big stain on it …'

Ralph suddenly had an idea.

'What if we turn the cushion over, so they don't notice the stain?' he suggested, putting the cushion back on the sofa upside-down and looking up proudly.

Ralph's mother frowned.

'Really, Ralph! We can't do that. The Monaghans are our friends. I suppose I had better ring Sarah's grandmother and tell her about the stain.'

Ralph paced up and down while his mother was on the phone to Sarah's grandmother. He felt even more nervous than he had the day he had to wait outside the headmaster's office after punching Bert.

'What did she say?' asked Ralph when his mother finally got off the phone.

'She said she has a wonderful stain remover that gets black marks out of just

about anything. You're very lucky, young
man.'

'I guess that's the last time I'll be allowed
to do my homework in front of the TV,'
said Ralph.

'I should say so!' said Ralph's mother,
ruffling his hair. 'In any case, no biros,

pencils,
crayons, textas,
permanent markers
or highlighters anywhere
near the new sofa, all right?'

'All right,' said Ralph, going back up to his room to finish his homework.

Neither Ralph nor his mother had seen the sleeping pencil or her new friends under the cushion. The five outcasts were blissfully unaware that the sofa they were trapped in would be moved to a new house the next day.

chapter 9

A Journey

Penny was enjoying a very pleasant dream. Ralph had just punched Bert the Bully in the nose, and Mrs Sword had punished him by making him write 'I must not punch big, mean bullies in class' 100 times. Penny was flying across the paper, writing the words in her neatest script.

'Slow down, Penny,' said Ralph giggling, his hand barely able to keep up with the speed she was writing at. 'Mrs Sword might notice!'

'Nearly finished,' said Penny, panting.

'I said slow down,' said Ralph again.

'I said put it down!' said a deep voice.

There was a bang and Penny felt the ground shake around her. She woke up screaming.

'Shhhh, it's okay,' said a familiar voice close to her. It was Stubbs.

'What's happening?' said Penny, feeling very frightened.

'I'm not sure,' said Stubbs, looking around anxiously. 'I think they're moving the sofa. Ralph's mum normally does it once a week or so when she vacuums. But this is different. Lead and Umbilica have gone to investigate.'

'You ready yet?' said a different deep voice from outside the cushions.

'Yeah,' said the original voice. 'Just had to wedge the door open. One, two, lift!'

Penny and Stubbs felt themselves being hoisted into the air and then they started to move forwards.

'Tilt it a bit to the left!' called the first deep voice, and Penny and Stubbs felt themselves roll deeper between the cushions.

'Look oooooooooout!' yelled a high-pitched voice, and Umbilica and Lead came rolling down to join them at high speed, only missing crashing into them by inches.

'What's happening?' asked Stubbs, once the other two had caught their breath.

'They're moving us outside, and I think they're going to put us into a big, green truck!' said Umbilica excitedly.

'Are Ralph and his mother moving house?' asked Stubbs.

'I don't think so,' said Lead. 'The truck isn't big enough for all the furniture. I think it's just this sofa.'

'No!' cried Penny in a panic. 'They can't

take us away from Ralph's house! What about Gloop? How are we going to save him from the textas?'

Umbilica rolled over to Penny. Her face was set.

'I'm sorry, Penny. It's like I said before. Once you're lost in the cushions, you're gone for good. We have exactly the same chance of helping Gloop now that we did before they moved the sofa out of Ralph's house.'

'But Gloop! We have to help him!' said Penny, pushing very hard against one of the cushions in a last, desperate attempt to escape from the sofa.

Penny was so full of adrenaline that she managed to push the cushion hard enough to make it start to fall off the sofa!

A ray of light appeared between the cushions and Penny rolled towards it as fast

as she could. As the cushion moved along, Penny rolled after it.

'Wee-heeeeee!' called a voice behind her, and Penny turned around just in time to see Zapper go hurtling past her. 'Free at laaaaaast!' he called, just before disappearing over the edge of the sofa.

'Hold on!' said one of the deep voices from outside the sofa, which Penny now realised belonged to a removal man. 'You just dropped something!'

'Where?' asked the second voice.

'Just near your foot. We'd better put the sofa down so you can pick it up!'

The two removal men tilted the sofa back the other way. Penny, who had been rolling towards the edge, now felt herself rolling in the other direction towards the backrest. She tried really hard to push herself upwards, but the material the sofa was made of was much harder to roll on than a table top, and she came to a complete standstill.

'Looky here! It's a TV remote control!' said the second removal man, picking up Zapper and looking at him closely. 'Better give that back!' he said, walking back into the house.

'Probably been lost in there for years!' muttered the first man. 'I wonder what else is under here?' he said, picking up the cushion next to Penny where Stubbs, Lead and Umbilica were. 'Well, well, well!' he said, seeing the broken bits of pencil. 'I don't think we'll be needing you,' he said, picking them up and throwing them on the ground. Each of them splintered into three or more pieces.

Penny was both horrified and excited. Although she wanted to escape from the sofa and get back to Gloop, the thought of making her way from the garden back into the house and finally into Ralph's pencil-case was quite daunting. That was if she even survived the fall! Penny screwed her eyes shut tightly as the man lifted up the cushion she was hiding under.

'Oh ho ho! What do we have here?' he said, spotting Penny. Penny felt hot, fat, sweaty fingers close around her and lift her

up into the air. If the man dropped her onto
the hard concrete below, she knew she'd end
up in even more pieces than Lead, Umbilica
and Stubbs.

'Quite a nice-looking pencil!' said the
first removal man, twisting Penny around
and eyeing her from every angle. 'You'll be
coming with me!' he said, shoving her into
his back pocket, just before his partner

arrived to help him carry the sofa into the truck and deliver it to Sarah's grandmother.

'All set?' said the first removal man to his partner.

'Yep! They were so pleased to have the remote control back. I get a real kick out of being nice to people, don't you?' he asked and started whistling.

'Yeah, I just love that warm, gooey feeling you get inside after you've helped someone in need,' said the first removal man sarcastically. But his partner was whistling so loudly he didn't notice the sarcastic tone of voice.

Penny didn't like the man who had stolen her at all. He seemed even nastier than Bert the Bully. His pocket smelled funny and his bottom vibrated in a funny way from time to time. Penny decided that she had to escape. Risking a long fall to the ground where she might shatter into pieces would be better than staying in the pocket of the horrible man. Penny started kicking at the stitching of the man's pocket, trying to dig a little hole in it. She was just starting to make some progress when she suddenly felt pressed in from all sides. Then there was a very different sort of vibration, and Penny realised that she and the men were in the green truck, about to drive off somewhere! She tried wriggling as hard as she could, but the man's bottom had wedged her in so tightly against the seat that she couldn't move an inch.

'Goodbye, Gloop,' she said sadly, as the truck gave a lurch and drove away from Ralph's house, the pencil-case and Penny's last chance of saving Gloop.

chapter 10

Breaking More Rules

Penny found the drive to her new home most unpleasant. Every now and again, the horrible man who had stolen her would wriggle his bottom around, pressing her against the seat even more tightly. Plus, those odd vibrations she had felt while he was walking happened again from time to time, and were always accompanied by a foul odour.

'What did you have for breakfast?' asked the second removal man. 'Baked beans on toast? A boiled egg?'

'Wife made a curry last night,' said the

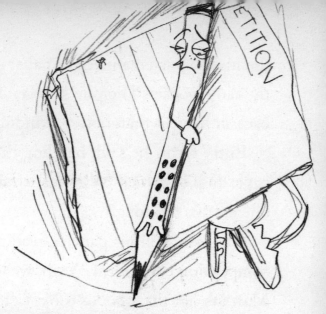

first. 'She's a great cook. Gonna enter the big cake baking competition tomorrow.'

'Which competition?' asked the second man.

'You know. The County Cake Baking Championship. Wife's been talking about nothing else for weeks,' said the first removal man, reaching into his back pocket where he had stashed Penny.

Penny felt the pressure ease off slightly, and suddenly felt herself lifted up a little as the man extracted a piece of paper out of the same pocket. Then he sat even further back in his seat than before, winding Penny.

'Entry form,' he said, handing the slip of paper to his partner. 'Wife made me pick one up this morning.'

'Oh, that,' said his partner, reading the competition entry form. 'Yeah, well, Martha's not that good a cook, to tell you the truth. And she says that since we both work, we can take it in turns to do the cooking. And the cleaning. I don't mind though. I'm all for this women's liberation business ...'

'Well whaddaya know! There already,' said the first removal man rudely, cutting his partner off mid-sentence. 'Let's drop this ugly sofa off quickly, then we can break early for lunch,' he said, snatching the entry form for the County Cake Baking

Championship from his partner and shoving it back in the pocket Penny was trapped in.

Penny felt the pressure ease off a second time as the man got out of the truck. That strange vibration happened again, pushing Penny and the competition entry form up out of the pocket slightly, and the air around her stank so badly that she could hardly breathe. That gave Penny an idea. Instead of trying to burrow her way out of a hole in the bottom of the man's pocket, she would try to push herself and the entry form out of the top of the pocket instead. That way, not only would she escape but the nasty man would get in trouble from his wife when he arrived home without it!

The men carried the sofa from the truck to the house and rang the front doorbell. As the door opened, the horrible smell Penny

was used to was replaced by the heavenly
smell of a freshly-baked cake.

'Hello, missy. Is your mother home?'
asked the nicer of the two men, who helped
his wife with the cooking and the cleaning.

'No. But my grandmother is,' said a voice
Penny recognised. 'She's just in the kitchen,
icing a cake. Are you the men with the sofa?'

'Yes we are,' said the nasty removal man impatiently, 'and it's rather heavy, so do you mind if we come in and put it down, little girl?'

'Of course,' said the little girl. Penny was trying to work out where she knew the voice from. It was so familiar … 'Granny wants it in the living-room.'

Penny peeked over the top of the pocket. The house looked very nice. Not expensively decorated, but cosy. As the men walked into the living-room Penny saw a school bag she recognised.

'Who's at the door, Sarah?' called an old woman's voice from the kitchen.

Sarah! Of course! This was Sarah's house! If only Penny could wriggle a bit further out of the pocket so that Sarah could see her …

'It's the men with the sofa, Granny,' replied Sarah.

'Ask them if they wouldn't mind bringing it into the living-room,' called Sarah's grandmother from the kitchen.

'Already have!' said Sarah proudly, earning a wink from the nicer of the two delivery men. Penny heard the nasty man groan, and struggled harder to wriggle to the top of the pocket to freedom, dragging the entry form with her.

Sarah's grandmother appeared in the doorway carrying a beautifully decorated cake: 'Just in time. You will stay for a slice of cake, won't you?'

'Well, we're kind of in a hurry …' began the nasty removal man, trailing off. 'Did you say cake?'

'Yes, I've just finished baking it!' said Sarah's grandmother.

'Well, we never say no to cake, do we?' said the man, walloping his partner on the shoulder.

'Please, take a seat on the sofa,' said Sarah's grandmother. 'After carrying it all this way, you deserve to at least sit on it!'

And just as Penny had made it to the top of the pocket, the nasty removal man slammed himself down on the sofa, wedging her in tight again.

'This cake is fabulous,' said the nicer removal man.

'You wouldn't have the recipe, would you?' asked the nasty man, unusually polite, thought Penny.

'Why, yes. Although I have to say, you don't really look like the cake baking type!' said Sarah's grandmother, going into the kitchen to get her recipe book.

'I'm not. But my wife loves to cook,' he called after her. Penny suddenly realised that the man had not only stolen her, he was planning to steal Sarah's grandmother's cake recipe so that his wife could win the County Cake Baking Championship!

Sarah's grandmother returned to the living-room, carrying the recipe book and a piece of paper. 'I'm sorry,' she said, 'but I couldn't find anything to write with. Sarah, be a dear and fetch your pencil-case.'

'No need,' said the nasty man, reaching into his back pocket and grabbing Penny, 'I have a pencil!'

As the man pulled Penny out of her pocket, she dragged the entry form with her, letting it drop behind one of the cushions. As the man started writing, Penny heard a gasp.

'That's Ralph's pencil!' said Sarah.

'I beg your pardon, Sarah,' said her grandmother.

'That's Ralph's favourite pencil!' said Sarah, staring angrily at the removal man. 'It's been missing for days. Ralph must have dropped it behind the sofa, and that man's gone and stolen it!'

'Oh-ho, Sarah!' laughed her grandmother. 'I'm sure there are lots of pencils that look like Ralph's favourite. You have one just like it, too!'

But Sarah wasn't convinced. She scowled at the nasty man as she chewed her cake. He narrowed his eyes back at her and kept writing.

Penny was pleased that Sarah had

recognised her. She couldn't believe how evil the man was – actually using a stolen pencil to steal a cake recipe! Penny knew what she had to do. It didn't matter now if she broke the rules and corrected the man's spelling, or in this case 'miscorrected' his spelling. Instead of '3 cups of self-raising flour', Penny wrote '2 cups of plain flour'. Instead of '1 teaspoon of vanilla essence' she wrote '1 tablespoon of hot mustard'. And instead of 'bake in a moderate oven for one hour' she wrote 'bake in a hot oven for an hour and a half'. By the time she had finished, Penny was quite pleased with herself.

'How much do I owe you?' asked Sarah's grandmother when the men had finished their cake.

'We didn't agree on a price in advance?' asked the nasty man slyly.

'Not that I remember …' said Sarah's grandmother.

The removal man smiled an evil grin. Sarah glowered at him suspiciously.

'In that case, since you gave us such a lovely slice of cake, we'll give you a discount off our usual price,' said the removal man. 'Why don't you go and warm up the

engine?'
he
suggested
to his
partner.
'You
mean I get to
drive?' said
his partner
excitedly.

'If you go now before I change my mind
…' said the nasty removal man impatiently.

'Brill!' said the nice removal man, taking
the keys off his partner and ruffling Sarah's
hair on the way out.

Once his partner was gone, the nasty
removal man used Penny to scribble out the
price on the bill of twenty-five euro, but
instead of writing a lower price, he tried to
write thirty euro! Penny realised in time and

forced him to write a '2' instead of a '3'. The man gave Sarah's grandmother the bill.

'There you go,' said Sarah's grandmother passing the man a twenty euro note.

The man stood with his hand out, expecting Sarah's grandmother to give him a second note. Sarah's grandmother raised her eyebrow.

'Young man, if you gave me a discount only to get a tip, then you have another thing coming!'

The man looked at his copy of the bill, and shook his head. He was sure he'd written thirty euro, but the figure on the bill clearly said twenty euro.

'Em … Yes … Of course. Good day,' he said, folding the money and putting Penny back in his pocket. There was a lot more room in the pocket without the entry form in there, and Penny desperately tried to wriggle up to the top. Before she could get far enough, the man was out of the house. Penny only managed to get her eyes above the top of the pocket in time to see the door closing on Sarah's scowling face.

chapter 11

Baking the Perfect Cake

'Now, let's get that stained cushion cover clean,' said Sarah's grandmother, steering Sarah back into the living-room. 'I'll run the water in the tub, and you get the cushion cover.'

Sarah stomped over to the sofa and wrenched the stained cushion off the seat. As she did so, the entry form for the County Cake Baking Championship flew up into the air. Sarah caught the piece of paper and read it.

'Granny!' she said, running into the laundry. 'There's the County Cake Baking

Championship tomorrow! The first prize is
five hundred euro. You should enter!'

Sarah's grandmother read the entry form,
looked at her watch, and shook her head
sadly. 'Sarah, I used the last of the baking
powder this morning and the shops are
about to shut …'

'I'll ride to the shop on my bike. I can
take a short-cut and get there even faster

than when you drive. Come on, Granny!'
said Sarah excitedly.

'Oh, I guess I may as well enter. Here,
take my purse,' said her grandmother. 'I'll
wash the mixing bowls and the cake tin,
and the kitchen will be all ready by the time
you get back.'

Sarah didn't waste a second. She jumped
on her bike and pedalled to the grocery
shop as fast as she could. As she rode past
McPaper's Books and Stationery Supplies
she noticed the display of coloured pencils
in the window.

'When Granny wins tomorrow I'll be
able to buy as many packets of coloured
pencils as I want!' she thought, pedalling
even faster. She got to the grocery shop just
before it closed and bought the last packet
of baking powder on the shelf.

Sarah arrived home quite out of breath.

Her grandmother had the kitchen looking spotless, with all the ingredients laid out neatly on the bench, waiting for the baking powder.

'Here you go,' said Sarah, putting the baking powder with the rest of the ingredients. She went around the other side of the bench and climbed onto the stool she always sat on while she watched her grandmother bake.

'What are you doing?' asked Sarah's grandmother.

'I'm watching you bake!' said Sarah, matter-of-factly.

'Oh, no you're not!' replied her grandmother. 'Have a look at the entry form!'

Sarah looked at the entry form. Her grandmother had

filled it out, but there was one mistake.

'Granny – you've made a mistake. You've written Sarah Monaghan instead of Gladys Monaghan.'

'It wasn't a mistake,' said her grandmother, with a funny smile on her face.

'What do you mean?' asked Sarah.

'I'm going to teach you how to bake. Goodness knows, if you're big enough to cycle to the shops and buy baking powder by yourself, you're big enough to bake a cake by yourself.'

'By myself?' said Sarah, imagining what her cake would look like: all lopsided and not cooked properly. She thought of the coloured pencils and her face fell.

'Don't worry. You'll be fine. And I'll help you, of course,' said her grandmother, handing Sarah an apron.

Sarah found that baking wasn't quite as difficult as she imagined. Her grandmother was very helpful, telling Sarah what to do, and she didn't make any mistakes.

'There!' said Sarah's grandmother as they put the cake in the oven. 'Now we wait for an hour,' she said setting the timer, 'and when the bell rings, your first place winning cake will be ready to come out of the oven.'

Sarah was very nervous. She spent the whole hour pacing the kitchen and must have looked in the oven one hundred times. Finally the timer rang.

'Gran-ny!' called Sarah. 'The cake's ready!'

'Shhh!' said her grandmother, coming into the kitchen. 'You don't want the cake to sink, do you?' Sarah's grandmother put on her oven gloves and took the cake out of the oven very carefully. She placed it on a

wire rack to cool. 'It looks lovely, Sarah.
We'll let it cool and then I'll help you ice
it.'

Sarah breathed a sigh of relief. She wasn't
very good at icing and would need her
grandmother's help if they were going to
win first place!

* * * *

On the other side of town, baking wasn't going so well. Penny had given up trying to get out of the nasty removal man's pocket and just had to put up with the constant vibrating and the disgusting smells. When the removal man finally got out of the truck and walked into what Penny assumed was his own house, instead of being greeted by the pleasant smell of baking that was at Sarah's house, Penny's nostrils were assaulted by the smell of burning.

'What's happening?' asked the removal man cautiously.

'Where have you been?' screamed a frazzled female voice.

'I told you I had a job this morning!' said the removal man, sounding a little apprehensive.

'Did you get me the entry form?' demanded the female voice. Being in the removal man's back pocket, Penny couldn't see the woman, but she assumed the woman was the removal man's wife.

'I did better than that!' he said, pulling the recipe Penny had miscopied for him out of another pocket. 'I got you the recipe for the perfect cake!'

'I have the recipe for the perfect cake already!' said the woman. 'See?' she said, thrusting a cake tin with a charred cake in it under her husband's nose.

'Now, Sugarpop, I know your cakes are … normally … delicious, but I had to deliver a sofa to an old lady this morning, and she'd just made the best cake I've ever tasted …' the removal man's voice trailed off as he saw his wife's face, '… equaled only by one of your … usual … masterpieces. What happened?'

'I don't know,' wailed his wife. 'I followed the recipe to the letter, set five different timers to make sure I'd take the cake out of the oven in time, but it's still burnt!' she said, throwing the burnt cake on the floor for emphasis.

'Look,' said the removal man somewhat nervously. 'Why don't you sit down and relax? I'll clean up the mess – I mean kitchen – and then you can try making this new recipe. The old woman was at least a hundred. If she can make a cake that's better than – I mean as good as one of yours – then you'll be able to do wonders with it. Won't you, Sugarpop?'

The removal man's wife glared at him for a moment, then snatched the recipe off him saying: 'Fine! Get me a margarita!'

She stomped into the living-room and flopped down on a chair. The removal man quickly made his wife the margarita and brought it to her. 'Interesting,' she murmured, taking the drink from him without looking up from the recipe. 'She uses plain flour instead of self-raising flour, and hot mustard! I didn't think you liked mustard!' said the removal man's wife accusingly.

'She put mustard in the cake? You really couldn't taste it …'

'And she cooks it for an hour and a half? Surely that's too long. Are you sure you copied this down correctly?'

'Yes, I'm sure I did, Sugarpop,' said the removal man through clenched teeth as he chiselled at the charred cake to get it out of the tin.

'Hmph!' said his wife. 'Let me know when you've finished in there, won't you?'

'Of course I will, Sugarpop,' said the man, barely able to control his temper. He felt a strange vibration coming from his back pocket. This time it had nothing to do with the curry he had eaten the night before but everything to do with the little pencil in there who was laughing at the evil removal man getting in trouble with his even more horrible wife!

chapter 12

A Surprise in the Night

Inside the pencil-case all the writing implements were sleeping, apart from Jade the short green pencil.

'Hey – Amber. Are you awake?' whispered Jade.

'Yes,' said Amber. 'I can't sleep. I keep wondering if Penny's okay.'

'Me too. There hasn't been an expulsion since Black Texta's Ethnink Cleansing. Now all the grey lead pencils are gone, how long do you think it will be before he starts expelling us coloured pencils?'

'Not at all, if I can help it,' said a deep

136

voice in the dark.

Amber and Jade opened their eyes wide
in alarm. They had no idea that anyone else
was awake and listening in to their
conversation, and it was forbidden to talk
after dark. They turned around slowly,
expecting to see a texta snarling down at
them, but to their surprise they saw Gloop!

'Gloop!' said Amber. 'What's happened
to you?'

Gloop was looking very healthy. His muscles had grown back and his label was all clean and shiny again. He was like a beacon of light in the dark.

'Black Texta set the Fright Permanent Marker on me,' said Gloop. 'But I'm feeling a lot better and stronger now. What were you saying about Penny?'

Amber and Jade looked at each other uneasily.

'Black Texta had her expelled,' said Jade.

'Ah,' said Gloop. 'On what grounds?'

'Helping Ralph with a sums test,' said Amber.

'Will she never learn?' said Gloop under his breath. 'When did this happen?'

'A couple of days ago,' began Jade. 'But that's not all ...'

'What else?' asked Gloop.

'Before they expelled her, they sharpened

her,' whispered Amber.

'Right,' said Gloop, turning angrily and marching towards the textas. He strolled right up to the sleeping Black Texta and tapped him in the side with his foot.

'Where is she?' said Gloop angrily.

Black Texta woke up startled, and then his eyes narrowed.

'Gloop? Is that you?' he said, sounding a little unsure of himself.

'Yes. Your little plan failed and now I'm your worst nightmare. Where is she?'

'Where's who?' said Black Texta, giving Rubber a kick to wake him up.

Rubber stirred, looking sleepy and chewing on something that looked suspiciously like a pencil

shaving. Gloop ripped it out of Rubber's jaws. He recognised the little round bubbles of Penny's skirt instantly.

'I'm not going to ask you again,' said Gloop, thrusting Penny's shaving under Black Texta's nose. 'Where is she?'

'I quite honestly haven't the faintest idea,' said Black Texta.

'What have you done with her?' said Gloop slowly.

'Nothing that she didn't have coming to her.'

The sound of the heated conversation had woken up all the other textas, pencils and crayons, who all gathered around to watch what was going on.

'What, exactly, did she have coming to her?' said Gloop.

'The usual penalty for disobeying the pencil-case rules. A second time,' said Black

Texta smugly, nodding at his texta henchmen, who started to close in around Gloop.

Gloop looked at the texta henchmen, but instead of cowering and backing off, he took a deep breath, making his chest and arm muscles swell. The texta henchmen looked a little scared and backed off.

'You expelled her?' said Gloop quietly.

'Oh, far worse than that. She helped Ralph cheat on a sums test, so I'm afraid we had to give her a sharpening,' said Black Texta, laughing evilly.

'You had to give her a sharpening,' said Gloop in disbelief. 'Was she blunt?'

'Amazingly so,' said Black Texta, nodding to his henchmen who started to close in on Gloop again.

'So, if she was blunt,' began Gloop, not at all worried about the advancing textas, 'how

did she manage to write on the test?'

The smug look disappeared from Black Texta's face.

'Erm ... well ...' he began, looking around desperately.

Gloop stared hard at Black Texta, then looked towards the advancing textas, who immediately backed off.

'It would be impossible for her to write if she were blunt, wouldn't it?' said Gloop, taking a step towards Black Texta. 'Kind of like a texta being able to write when it has lost its cap and the ink has gone dry.'

Gloop shot his hands forward and pulled at Black Texta's cap. Black Texta held onto his cap tightly and tried to pull away from

Gloop.

'Get him, boy,'
he yelled to Rubber.

Rubber snapped at
Gloop's ankles, but
Gloop kicked him away
without letting go of
Black Texta's cap. Black Texta backed away
from Gloop until he hit the wall of the
pencil-case. With nowhere else to go, and
without Rubber or the textas to help him,
there was nothing more Black Texta could
do. His cap started to come off slowly ...
slowly ... until there was a loud POP and
Black Texta's tip was exposed.

'Hey, Fido,' called Gloop, tossing the cap
out of the open zipper. 'Go fetch!'

Rubber went bounding after the cap,
leaping over the zip before he realised it was
too late.

Gloop turned his attention back to Black Texta. 'Where was the pencil-case when you expelled Penny?' he asked.

Black Texta didn't answer, but smiled a weak, yet evil, grin back at Gloop.

'This is your last chance. I won't ask you again. Where was the pencil-case when you expelled Penny?' Gloop demanded.

Black Texta chuckled.

'On Ralph's sofa,' said Black Texta weakly.

Satisfied, Gloop nodded and turned away.

'But it won't do you any good,' called Black Texta, making Gloop stop in his tracks and turn around. 'Ralph's mum sold the sofa. It was taken away this morning.'

'What?' said Gloop.

Black Texta smiled evilly.

'While you were sleeping a green van came and took your precious Penny away from you.'

Gloop's clean label seemed to lose some of its gleam.

'So you see, all of your heroics were for nothing.'

Gloop turned to Jade and Amber.

'Is that true?' he asked.

'I'm afraid so,' said Jade. 'Went about 11 o'clock.'

'Looks like I've triumphed over you again,' said Black Texta nastily, 'you do-goody bottle of correction fluid. You can't correct everything now, can you?'

Gloop looked at the ground and shook his head sadly.

'You there! Purple!' commanded Black Texta. 'Give me your cap!'

Gloop snapped his head up. 'Stop!' he said.

The purple texta paused with his hands at the base of his cap.

'You take that cap off, and what do you

think will happen to you?' said Gloop.

The purple texta hesitated.

'You'll dry up, that's what,' said Gloop. 'Do you think Black Texta would do the same for you?' he said, turning to the rest of the textas. 'For any of you?'

Slowly all the textas began to shake their heads. Purple took his hands away from his cap and looked at Black Texta with disgust.

The pencils and crayons all looked at Gloop with renewed admiration.

'Are you going to expel him?' asked Pink Crayon excitedly.

'I'll leave that up to him,' said Gloop, looking at Black Texta. 'He's all dried up anyway.'

Gloop turned away from Black Texta and looked around the pencil-case. 'Come on. We've got a lot of work to do to be ready in time for school on Monday.'

chapter 13

On the Road Again

Penny found it very difficult to wake up the
next morning. She wasn't feeling very well
after all the foul air she'd been inhaling and
she was still feeling a bit seasick from all
the weird vibrations in the nasty removal
man's trousers the day before. Plus, she
hadn't had much sleep. It seemed that the
removal man and his wife had been up
more than half the night, screaming at each
other and baking cake after cake, then
screaming at each other again as each cake
came out of the oven a disaster. At first
Penny was quite proud of herself for having

miscopied Sarah's grandmother's secret
recipe. But when she woke up that morning
feeling very ill indeed, she was wondering if
it had really been such a good idea. Her
whole body ached and she had a very bad
headache.

As the removal man pulled on his
trousers from the day before, Penny

wondered if she could really stand another day of bad smells and motion sickness. She worked her way to the top of the pocket and had every intention of throwing herself out of it onto the polished floorboards below. She'd be sure to shatter into a million pieces. Before she could get all the way out of the pocket, the man started walking. As he moved his leg forward, the material on the pocket stretched tightly, trapping Penny.

After a few paces the man stopped walking, and said in a delicate voice: 'Aw, that looks fabulous, Sugarpop!'

'It took me until 4am, but I think we have a winner here,' said his wife, in a much calmer voice than anything Penny had heard her say the day before.

'I'll just go and start the car ...' began the removal man.

'Oh, no you won't!' said his wife, in the voice that Penny was used to.

'Why not? It's quite a long drive, and we've only got ...'

'You're not going to drive me to the County Cake Baking Championship wearing those dirty trousers!' she said. 'Go and change them at once! We have to go.'

'Yes, Sugarpop,' said the removal man, turning around to walk back to the bedroom to change his trousers.

As he did so, Penny's heart sank. From the top of the pocket she was able to glance at the kitchen table, and sitting there on a lovely presentation tray was a cake that looked every bit as good as Sarah's grandmother's!

The removal man muttered to himself all the way to the bedroom, took his trousers off and threw them on the floor. Penny breathed a sigh of relief. She wouldn't have to spend another day putting up with the vibrations and the smells. The material of the trousers made a little cocoon around Penny, and she felt safe and warm. It reminded her of something … what was it? Something like … the inside of Ralph's pencil-case. Yes, that was it. Except it wasn't so crowded without all the coloured pencils and textas and Gloop …

Gloop! In all the excitement of yesterday Penny had completely forgotten about the need to save her friend! Through the material of the trousers Penny could hear the faint sound of car keys clinking as the removal man picked them up off the bed-side table, followed by the dull thud of heavy shoes walking out of the bedroom.

'No! Come back! You've forgotten me!' called Penny, but the sound of the shoes faded away as the removal man walked out of the bedroom.

'I've got to get to the County Cake Baking Championship!' said Penny, trying to crawl out of the pocket. 'Sarah will be there. She will have found the entry form and convinced her grandmother to bake another cake, and when she sees me she'll recognise me and take me back to Ralph ...'

The weight of the trouser material was very heavy and Penny found it very hard to move. She struggled and struggled until at last she broke free of the trousers. She looked around her and saw the door leading to the hallway. The wooden floorboards were even easier to roll on than a table top, and in no time at all Penny had made it down the hall and into the kitchen, just in time to see the removal man's wife walk out the door carrying the cake.

'Nooo!' yelled Penny, rolling across the kitchen floor at full speed as the door was closing. Just as Penny made contact with the door it slammed shut. The impact knocked Penny up on one end. As her head crashed into the bottom of the door, her toe flew into the air and she did a complete cartwheel before colliding with the door a second time. But Penny's foot didn't stop when it should have. It kept on moving, pushing the door with it. This bit of the door wasn't cold and hard like the bit Penny had hit her head on, it was rubbery and flexible … a cat flap! Penny suddenly found herself outside on the front porch, squinting in the sunlight.

Penny blinked a few times and looked around. There was a car at the end of the driveway and the removal man's wife was very carefully laying the cake on the back seat before shutting the door and getting into the front passenger seat. That would take about ten seconds. Penny had a chance!

She gave herself a push, rolled towards the steps, and stopped short. It was a long way down from the top of one step to another, and there were six steps in all. Unlike her fall out of the pencil-case onto soft cushions, there was only hard concrete

beneath her.
Penny looked
over the edge
and shuddered.
She thought of
Lead, Umbilica
and Stubbs, and
what had happened to
them when they'd landed on the concrete.
She heard a second car door slam, thought
of Gloop, then gave herself a hard shove.

She rolled over the edge and hit her
cheek on the first step, bruised her hip on
the second, landed flat on her face on the
third step, bounced on the top of her head
on the fourth step, and completely missed
the fifth step to land painfully on the
concrete path below.

Penny heard the car engine roar into life.
She was dizzy and dazed, but she followed

her instinct and rolled towards the noise of the car as fast as she could. She felt her head hit something fairly soft, and her leg flew into the air again. This time her foot slammed into something hard and got stuck there. Penny felt her body whirling around faster and faster, and felt very seasick indeed. After what seemed like hours the spinning stopped, and Penny heard somebody laughing at her.

'Feeling a bit dizzy, are we?' said a deep voice.

Penny's head was spinning, and when she opened her eyes it looked like there were ten lions looking at her and laughing.

'A little dizzy ...' she said. 'Who are all of you?'

'All of us?' said the same voice. 'There's only one of me! You must be dizzy ...'

As the voice continued speaking, some of

the lions started to disappear and merge into one.

'What's happeniiiiiiiiiiiing?' said Penny, as the noise of the car engine increased and the whirling started again. Luckily, as soon as it had started, the whirling stopped. Penny looked around and saw six lions. They eventually merged into one.

'Traffic jam,' said the single lion. 'Looks like we'll be bumping into each other a bit along the next stretch of road.'

'Who did you say you were?' said Penny, trying to clear her head.

'Oh, how rude of me. I'm Leo. Standard hubcap embossment for all 1998 model 5 Chiceras. And what on Earth are you?'

'I'm a pencilllllllllllllllll,' explained Penny, as the whirling started a third time. The car stopped again and Leo pulled up alongside Penny.

'A pencil?' asked four Leos at once. 'What does a pencil do?' Penny waited until the images had blended into a single Leo before explaining.

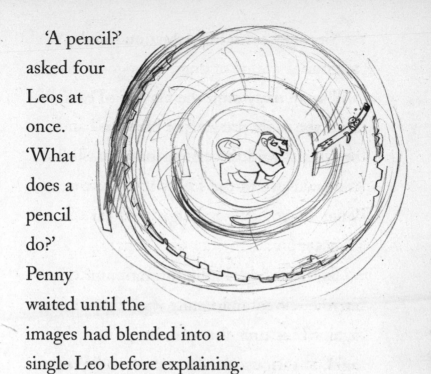

'I write. A human picks me up, moves me across paper, and lead comes out of my toe, leaving words behind on the paper. What about yoooooou …' Again the car engine revved and Penny felt herself tumbling around and around. The vibrations from the removal man's trousers didn't feel anything like this!

'I protect tyres from the unwanted territorial waters of dogs. One good roar will scare away even the biggest of canines with the most pressing of bladder problems!' said three Leos proudly. 'Tell me,' said two of the Leos, 'if you're a pencil, what are you doing wedged in a car hubcap?'

'Is that where I ammmmmmmm?' The engine revved and Penny was off spinning again. This time the spinning continued for ages, at various speeds, and when the car finally stopped, Leo was nowhere to be seen.

It took Penny a while to realise that the engine had stopped humming completely. She heard a car door open and saw a foot appear. It was the foot Penny had seen disappearing through the closing kitchen door, belonging to the removal man's wife.

As the foot started walking away from her
Penny tried to wriggle free of the hubcap,
but her toe was jammed so
firmly she was unable to
move.

'How did you enjoy the journey, my
beautiful baby?' cooed the removal man's
wife, opening the back door and examining

the cake. 'Perfectly!' she said to herself with satisfaction, then picked the cake up and slammed the car door before walking off with her husband towards a big building. The slamming door was just enough to dislodge Penny's toe from the hubcap, and she fell down head-first onto the gravel below.

Penny felt very weak. After numerous bumps on the head and whirling around on the car's hubcap she was feeling even worse than she had when she first woke up. Penny tried desperately to roll through the gravel in the direction of the removal man and his wife, but with every push she sank lower and lower into the gravel.

Another car pulled up alongside Penny. She heard a door open and a pair of feet landed just inches from her.

'What's that I almost stepped on?' said a

kind voice. Penny felt a thumb and
forefinger close around her and pick her up.
'My, my! Somebody's lost their pencil. I'd
better drop this into the lost and found!'

The gentle crunch, crunch of the gravel
under the feet of the woman who had
picked her up lulled Penny into a much-
needed sleep.

chapter 14

The County Cake-Baking Championship

'Now don't take your seatbelt off until I come around and take the cake off your lap, Sarah. We don't want any of the icing to rub against the side of the container!'

'No, Granny,' said Sarah, sitting very still. She'd nursed the cake very carefully all the way from home to the hall where the County Cake Baking Championship was being held, and she definitely didn't want anything to go wrong at the last minute! Sarah's grandmother opened the door and took the cake gently off her lap. Sarah's

hands were trembling as she undid her
seatbelt.

'Maybe I should carry the cake into the
hall,' suggested Sarah's grandmother.

Sarah nodded and breathed a sigh of
relief.

There was quite a queue of people who
were holding all sorts of cake containers at
the entrance to the town hall. There were
plastic containers, tin containers, and some
brave people were even holding their cakes
on a plate with only cling wrap over the

top! Sarah and her grandmother had to wait
in the queue for quite a while. Sarah got
more and more nervous, and was sure that
she would have dropped the cake had she
been holding it!

Finally they got to the registration desk.
The lady smiled at them and took the entry
form.

'Gladys! It's been a while since we last saw you here. It's great to see you entering again,' said the registration lady.

'I'm not actually entering,' said Sarah's grandmother. 'I'm here with my grand-daughter Sarah.'

'Oh,' said the registration lady. 'Well, Sarah, if you can bake half as well as your grandmother, you're in with a good shot. Your cake is number 105. Good luck.'

The lady handed Sarah the number 105 and a map showing her which table inside the hall she should display her cake on.

Sarah and her grandmother walked into the hall. They found Table 105 with only a little difficulty. Sarah's grandmother took the cover off their plastic cake carrier and turned it upside-down. Then she placed the cake on top of the cover. It looked fantastic! Sarah was sure that if they didn't win, they'd at least come second or third.

'Let's go have a look at the other cakes!' said Sarah's grandmother. She was a very keen cook and always on the lookout for new baking ideas, although unlike the removal man, she would never even dream of stealing a recipe from someone else!

As they passed Table 98 there was quite a kerfuffle. A man and his wife were arguing loudly.

'I told you to pick up an entry form yesterday!'

'I did pick one up! I must have left it in

my trouser pocket. If you hadn't insisted on my changing …'

'I'm not having you wear your dirty old moving trousers to the County Cake Baking Championship! How will it look when I win first prize, if my husband hasn't even made the effort to dress nicely? Not that there's much chance of us winning with our cake on a table all the way back here. What's the point in getting here early if we have to waste time filling out the entry form and miss out on all the best tables …'

The noise caught Sarah's attention. She looked around and saw the removal man who had stolen Ralph's pencil. And that horrible woman he was arguing with must be his wife. Sarah was about to point this out to her grandmother when she saw the cake. It was identical to the one she and her grandmother had baked!

'Look, Granny!' said Sarah urgently,
tugging on her grandmother's sleeve. 'It's
the man who delivered our sofa yesterday.
And he's cheated by using your cake recipe!
Look!'

Sarah's grandmother looked over to
where Sarah was pointing and her eyes
narrowed.

'Tsk, tsk!' she said. 'I thought there was
something funny about him yesterday, when
he was waiting around for a tip. As if a slice
of my cake wasn't payment enough! And he
had the nerve to copy my cake recipe!'

'And he stole Ralph's pencil!' said Sarah,
glad that her grandmother finally agreed
that the removal man was dodgy.

Sarah's grandmother tilted her head on
an angle to get a better look at the cake.

'I don't think we need to worry too much,'

she said. 'The proof of the pudding's in the eating, and there's a special secret ingredient that I always add, that isn't in the recipe.'

'You mean the …'

'Shhhh!' said Sarah's grandmother. 'We don't want anyone else around here to hear.'

At that moment a voice came over the loud speaker: 'Ladies and gentlemen, welcome to the County Cake Baking Championship. Judging is about to begin.

Would those of you who have gone to
check out the competition please return to
your cakes. If you are not with your cake
when the judges arrive, you will be
automatically disqualified.'

'Quick, Granny! We have to go to our
cake table for judging!' said Sarah, pulling
her grandmother back to Table 105.

From Table 105 Sarah and her

grandmother had a clear view of Table 98. They noticed a few people on the tables in between pointing from their cake to the cake on Table 98. Sarah no longer felt nervous, but very angry. The judges would go to Table 98 before getting to Table 105, and they would think that she and her grandmother had copied the removal man and his wife, when really it was the other way around!

Eventually the judges got to Table 98.

'Oh, my! That's a fine-looking cake!' said the male judge.

'You've done yourself proud again this year, Muriel,' said the female judge.

'Ten out of ten for presentation!' said the male judge. 'Now for the taste-testing …'

He poked something that looked like a thin apple corer into the cake. When he pulled it back out, it had a tiny sliver of cake on it.

'Ladies first!' he said, offering it to the female judge. She took half the sliver of cake in her fingers, tilted her head back, and dropped the cake into her mouth. She immediately started coughing. The male judge thumped her on the back.

'Went down the wrong way, did it?' he asked.

The female judge whirled around and grabbed his arm.

'Stop hitting me on the back and try the cake yourself!' she said. Her face was red and her eyes were watering, and she looked as though she had eaten something she

really didn't like the taste
of.

The male judge
popped the rest of the
sliver of cake into his mouth.
He, too, started coughing.

The removal man and his wife
looked from one judge to the
other.

'What's wrong with the cake?'
demanded the wife.

'It gets a ten for presentation,
but minus marks for flavour,' said
the male judge angrily. 'Final score:
three out of twenty.'

'Three out of twenty?!' the removal man's
wife exploded. 'How can you give me minus
seven for flavour!'

'Have you tasted the cake yourself,
Muriel?' asked the female judge.

'Well, no … I …'

'Then I suggest you do, and I'm sure you'll agree that minus seven is quite a generous mark for something that tastes that bad!'

The judges turned on their heel and went on to the next table. The removal man's wife picked up the cake, turned to her husband and threw the cake at his face. The rest of the hall erupted in laughter. Sarah looked up at her grandmother, who gave her a knowing wink.

'It looks like those two got their just desserts!' she said.

A few minutes later the judges arrived at Table 105.

'Oh, no!' whispered the female judge to the male judge. 'It's the same sort of cake that Muriel baked. I really don't want to have to taste it again …'

'I think you'll find,' began Sarah's grand-mother loudly, 'that this cake tastes far superior to the one on Table 98. It is a family

recipe that my grandmother taught me, and my granddaughter did a splendid job of baking yesterday.'

The female judge was lost for words. Sarah had never seen her grandmother talk to anyone like that (other than when she told Sarah off for making a mess or leaving her homework until the last minute).

The male judge poked the skinny apple corer into the cake before Sarah's grandmother could say anything to him. He held his breath and put a small piece of the sliver of cake into his mouth. All of a sudden his face broke into a wide smile, and he went back for seconds!

'I think Sarah and her grandmother deserve a ten out of ten for presentation and flavour! What do you think?' the male judge asked his female partner.

The female judge looked at him distrustfully and took a small sliver of cake. As soon as she popped it into her mouth she started smiling too.

'Yes, I believe we may have found a winner here!' she said, writing two big fat tens next to Table 105 on her score sheet.

Sarah looked at her grandmother and smiled. Then she looked over to Table 98.

The removal man's wife was stomping out
of the hall, while the removal man, whose
face was covered in cake, was picking up the

cake carrier and running after her.

The judges moved on to sample the
remaining cakes to find out who would
come second and third.

Finally at two o'clock they were ready to
make the official announcement.

'First of all, we'd like to thank you all for coming here today, and for presenting your marvellous cakes. It's always a pleasure to judge a competition of such high quality,' said the male judge, patting his ample belly.

'We have some very talented bakers here in Hedgehog County, and we'd like to congratulate you all,' said the female judge.

'Now, without further ado, the placings for this year's County Cake Baking Championship!' said the male judge.

'Third prize goes to Jenny Williams!'

'Second prize goes to Carol North!'

'And first prize goes to someone who we believe is our youngest entrant ever, Sarah Monaghan!'

Even though she'd finally heard her name announced over the loudspeaker, Sarah still couldn't believe it. Her grandmother gave her a big hug. Suddenly there were people

crowding around her, taking photos and
asking questions.

'How long have you been baking cakes?'

'What ingredients did you use?'

'How are you going to spend the five
hundred euro?'

'Are you looking forward to telling
everyone at school tomorrow?'

By the time Sarah had finished
answering all their questions and having her
picture taken with the cake, she and her
grandmother were the last people left in the

181

hall, apart from the caretaker. Just as they got to the door to the carpark, the caretaker came running up to them. 'Excuse me!' he said.

Sarah and her grandmother turned around.

'Did one of you ladies lose a pencil?' he asked. 'It's the last thing left in the Lost and Found box. If it isn't yours, you may as well take it anyway.'

The caretaker held a hand out to them. As he uncurled his fingers Sarah recognised Ralph's pencil instantly.

'Granny! It's Ralph's pencil! That horrible removal man must have dropped it!' said Sarah excitedly.

'Thank you very much,' said Sarah's grandmother to the caretaker, taking Penny from him and passing her to Sarah. 'It's not actually our pencil, but my granddaughter is

very good friends with the little boy it
belongs to.'

Sarah closed her fingers tightly around
Penny to make sure she wouldn't get lost
again. Penny, who was still sleeping soundly,
nestled into the warm fingers and dreamed
pleasant dreams of dancing over pages and
pages of neatly ruled lines.

chapter 15

Home at Last

As soon as Sarah got home, she went straight to her pencil-case and put Penny in there for safe keeping. The sound of the zip closing woke Penny up. Just like her adventure behind the cushions, the first thing she became aware of was the sound of hushed voices whispering around her.

'Do you think that's really her?'

'It looks like her. I mean, it's the right colour, and although the tip's snapped off, it looks recently sharpened ...'

'The toe looks a bit mangled ...'

'What do you mean "The toe looks a bit

mangled"?' demanded Penny once she
realised the voices were talking about her.

'Er … well … not mangled as though
somebody had a big chew on you,' said the
third voice, sounding a little intimidated.
'It's just that your toe just looks a little … a
little … well … squashed.'

'Kind of like someone who didn't know
what they were doing tried to sharpen you
with a Stanley knife,' suggested one of the

other voices timidly. Everyone drew in their
breath at the word 'sharpen'.

Penny looked down at her toe. There was
a scar on either side of her ankle where the
hubcap had cut into her. She tried
wriggling her toe and it hurt a bit.

'So are you really Penny?' one of the
voices asked.

'Yes, I am. Who are all of you?'

'We're Sarah's pens and pencils!' said a chorus of writing implements.

'Sarah? Ralph's friend Sarah? You mean, she found me?' asked Penny, with tears in her eyes.

'Absolutely,' said a pencil that looked remarkably like Penny, but without the scars on her ankles. 'By the way, I'm Polly.'

'Will Sarah be taking us to school tomorrow?' asked Penny, hardly daring to believe that she would get to see Ralph and all his writing implements the next day.

'Of course! Sarah's already packed her school bag. At eight o'clock tomorrow morning we'll be on our way!'

'And I can come too?' asked Penny.

'Of course you can come too!' said Polly. 'What makes you think you won't be coming with us?'

Penny hesitated a moment. 'It's just that, well, the textas in Ralph's pencil-case expelled me …'

'Oh, them!' huffed Polly.

'What do you mean "oh them"?' asked Penny.

'Gloop has dealt with them. They won't be causing anyone any trouble any more,' said Polly knowingly.

'Gloop …?' began Penny.

'Yes, it's amazing what he's achieved! He used to be quite a lively little fellow, the IIC of Ralph's pencil-case …'

'IIC?' asked Penny.

'Yes. Implement In Command,' explained Polly. 'Managed to run a very tight pencil-case. The pencils all kept themselves sharpened, never went missing. The whole set-up was very efficient.'

'You mean Gloop used to boss all the

other pencils around?' asked Penny. 'Is that why nobody likes him?'

'Oh, no!' said Polly. 'The other pencils didn't dislike Gloop. They were just angry at him because he allowed himself to be overthrown by Black Texta. Unlike Black Texta, Gloop was a very fair ruler. Not a real ruler of course, because he's a bottle of correction fluid, but you know what I mean. He listened to what everyone had to say,

and didn't discriminate based on colour.
Everyone worked as a big, happy team.

'Black Texta on the other hand was an
autocrat. He was very mean, and wouldn't
listen to anybody. If anybody else seemed to
be becoming too popular, either with Ralph
or the other writing implements, he'd use
his spies to spread nasty rumours about them,
or think of a way to have them expelled.'

Penny wondered why Gloop had never
told her any of this. Maybe he thought she
wouldn't have believed him.

'How did Black Texta take over?' Penny
asked.

'You see, shortly after the textas arrived, there was a big battle between Gloop and Black Texta. Black Texta was purposefully making mistakes, and Ralph kept on using more and more of Gloop to white out the mistakes. Gloop became very weak and that's when Black Texta took over. He managed to turn all the other pens and pencils against Gloop, and used his texta army and that evil little Rubber to keep the others all living in fear.'

'So how did Gloop manage to get rid of him?' asked Penny.

'Apparently you had a lot to do with it,' said Polly, smiling at Penny.

'Me?' said Penny.

'Yes, you. Your devotion to Ralph and quality written work reminded Gloop a lot of himself in his younger days. He remembered what it was like to be young, and have hope, and thought it was sad that all the other writing implements were living under a regime of terror instead of living in harmony.'

'Oh,' said Penny.

'The night that Black Texta expelled you was the real turning point,' continued Polly. 'Black Texta made the mistake of using a permanent marker to subdue Gloop. Although it made Gloop weak and unconscious at first, the inky vapours were exactly what Gloop needed to become strong again. A few days later he and Black Texta had another gigantic battle. Gloop managed to get Black Texta's cap off him and threw it out of the pencil-case. It only took a short while before Black Texta dried up.'

'But what about Rubber and all the other textas?' asked Penny.

'Rubber, the obedient little lap dog that he was, jumped out of the pencil-case to fetch Black Texta's cap. He hasn't been seen since. As for the rest of the textas, Gloop threatened to do the same to them unless they learned to play nicely with the other writing implements.'

'So everyone's happy in Ralph's pencil-case now?' asked Penny.

'Oh yes. Much happier. Now that they know how tough life can be, they're really pleased to have Gloop back in charge. I'm sure they'll be happy to see you again. I know Gloop will be. He feels personally responsible for what happened to you.'

Penny lay quietly for a very long time. Imagine that! She thought she'd have to save Gloop, when really he was the one who thought he'd have to save her. That night she had very pleasant dreams indeed.

The next morning Penny was awoken by a sharp jolt. 'What was that?' she asked.

'Just Sarah picking up her school bag. Not long now and you'll be back in your own pencil-case,' said Polly.

Penny could hardly wait. Although all the writing implements in Sarah's pencil-case had been friendly to her since she arrived, she was excited about seeing Ralph's pencil-case the way Gloop had described it before the textas came: pencils playing with crayons, and everyone being friends.

After a lot of movement the zip opened and Penny heard Sarah's voice saying:

'Ralph! Look what I found.'

Sarah's little fingers entered the pencil-case and pushed all the other writing implements aside until she found Penny.

'My favourite pencil!' said Ralph, closing his fingers around Penny and kissing her. 'I

thought I'd lost this forever. Where did you find it?'

'Under the cushions of the sofa your mum gave away,' said Sarah, leaving out the unnecessary explanation involving the horrible removal man and his even more horrible wife.

'Cool!' said Ralph, using Penny to write his name and the date on the top of his paper. Penny obediently followed all the movements of Ralph's hand, and was pleased to see that his spelling had improved in the time she had been away.

By the time the bell went, Penny was even more excited about break-time than the children in class. She was very eager to see Gloop and all the happy writing implements in Ralph's pencil-case. After what must have been at least three full pages of writing, Ralph finally packed up his books, opened the zip to his pencil-case and dropped Penny inside.

'Welcome back!' cried all the pencils, crayons, textas, permanent markers, highlighters, and a new family of friendly-looking rubbers in the pencil-case. There were balloons and streamers, and a group of crayons had got together to make a very colourful sign saying 'Welcome home Penny!'

'It's good to be home,' said Penny,
looking at all the smiling faces around her.
Even the textas were pleased to see her. 'But
where's Gloop?'

A purple and yellow texta who were
standing next to each other took a step to
the side, and Gloop appeared between
them. Penny hardly recognised him at first.
He was so big and strong and shiny.

'Gloop, is that really you?' said Penny.
Gloop nodded.

'I'm so glad to see you …' they began

together.

'Oh, you go first,' said Penny.

'No, you go first,' said Gloop.

'Okay,' they began together. 'I thought Black Texta had …' they said, then stopped and waited for the other to speak.

'But it seems you didn't need my help …' they started together again, then burst out laughing.

'It's so good to have you home,' said Gloop.

'It's good to be home,' said Penny.

'And you know what the best bit is?' said one of the new little rubbers, jumping up

and down for attention. 'Ralph is so good at spelling and sums now, he hardly needs to use us at all!'

'So things have worked out well all round then,' said Penny.

'They have indeed,' said Gloop.

All the other writing implements cheered in agreement.

It really was good to be home.